Alfreda Vail, who had come to New York to work in the office of a cereal company, was looking for two apartment mates. The first two to answer her newspaper ad were Torre Sherrill, a glamorous brunette who looked like a movie star but was primarily interested in architecture; and Cindy Lamson, sometime blonde model whose chief aim in life was to find an attractive and wealthy husband.

Together, the three attempted to work out the complications of their individual careers and romances, occasionally crossing wires, and in the meantime drinking in the excitement, thrill and adventure which New York held.

THE "NEW" VEDA VAIL

THE "NEW" VEDA VAIL

by

JEAN CAREW

PRESTIGE BOOKS
NEW YORK, NEW YORK

To the success of

THE NEW YORK WORLD'S FAIR

Prestige Books, Inc.
18 East 41st Street, New York, New York 10017

Printed in the United States of America

THE "NEW" VEDA VAIL

Chapter 1

Alfreda Vail stood in the center of the room—the living room of the apartment she had rented—and looked around with distaste. The furniture was obviously shiny-new and lacking in any distinction. The maple finish and serviceable, dun-colored upholstery looked inconsequential and uninviting against the painted cream-colored walls; the brown carpet was thin and uninteresting.

Guaranteed to last eighteen months anyway, Alfreda thought gloomily, or they wouldn't get the final installment. She wondered what Reba Waters, the wife of the building superintendent, would say if she spoke aloud.

But the short, sturdy woman did not have the same point of view. "I think it looks real nice," she said. "Of course it's got to get mussed up a little before it'll look real good, and then maybe if you got some flowered drapes—"

Sam Waters, wrench in hand, came into the living

room from the bathroom. He was a big, heavy man, but he moved sluggishly, as if every step were an effort. His working uniform consisted of a tieless shirt, an open vest and baggy wrinkled pants, all topped by a striped cap. But his expression was kind as he looked at the young girl standing so forlornly in the middle of the room.

"Your hot water faucet is okay now," he assured her. "When was you expecting your friends?"

"When?" Alfreda had been toying with the thought of walking out of the miserable apartment and out of the miserable city of New York and returning to the friendly, warm atmosphere of her home in Kansas City.

"Oh, they'll be here this afternoon—or at least one of them," Alfreda stammered. For a moment she was tempted to tell Reba and Sam that her "friends" were purely imaginary; she expected only to have at least one answer to her ad. But in her present state of depression, she wondered if anyone at all would come.

The superintendent's wife seemed to sense her mood and said soothingly:

"Don't worry about the apartment, dearie. It will look fine when you get a few cushions and maybe a throw-rug or two around. I wish I could start with everything new in my place," she added meaningly to her husband.

"We'd better be gettin' back downstairs," Sam said

stolidly. "Call us if you need anything."

After they had left, Alfreda walked over and looked out at the deserted street. The East Seventies on a Sunday morning were deserted; the pavement glistened from last night's rain, and an awning flapped lonesomely on the apartment house across the way. She turned and walked resolutely through the living room and into the bedroom, assailed again by doubts as to the wisdom of what she was doing.

When the Right-O! Cereal Company of Kansas City had told her about the opening in the New York office, Alfreda's father had urged her to make the change. She needed to get away from the routine of keeping house for her old Dad and working, he insisted. It would be good for her to live in New York for a while, especially at a time when New York would be a mecca for those who wanted to see the glamorous, history-making World's Fair.

So Alfreda had come East. But there had been unexpected problems. Living in New York was expensive —far more expensive than it appeared from the viewpoint of a comfortable, well-established home in Kansas City. The Right-O! Cereal people had been generous in the matter of salary, but with living expenses so high, it was impossible to save anything, and Alfreda felt that was a shiftless way to exist.

The idea of renting an unfurnished apartment and advertising for roommates had been born of reading the

12

ads: "Apartments to Share." When she answered some ads, Alfreda had discovered "sharing" meant sharing the cost, but none of the privileges, of the lease holder. Among others, there was the woman who offered her the bedroom, but expected her to stay in it, because she used the living room for entertaining. Then there was the couple with two young children and a bathroom festooned with dozens of drying diapers. There had been one nice apartment, much like this, but another girl had moved in five minutes before Alfreda answered the ad.

The idea of renting an apartment herself and getting out of town girls to share it had been born right then. She had written her father, asking if he could send some furniture, but Dad, more practical, had offered to arrange credit and make the first payment on furniture ordered from a New York store. Alfreda had felt honor bound to be economical, but she found the result depressing.

She glanced into the bathroom. It was sparkling clean, but she would have to get more towels. The tiny hall also opened into the bedroom; this was so small the bed, bureau and chair gave it a fully furnished look. Beyond it, the dressing room, with a narrow window looking onto a court, was crowded. The small cot was just a few feet away from the really generous closet. Alfreda was thankful, in the interests of space, that the closet had folding doors.

"Anyway, it's clean and new," she muttered defensively to herself. "If nobody answers the ad—" At that moment the doorbell rang in three sharp, staccato blips of sound.

Nicholas Tyler strode purposefully along the Sunday-quiet streets, noting with approval the nice neighborhood. The number he was looking for appeared to be a well-kept apartment house; the lobby he entered was clean, if not spacious, and the elevators faced the street. They were the self-service variety, he saw, and frowned. Simon Sherrill probably wanted doormen for his beloved granddaughter; Nicholas Tyler's irritation at his errand and the necessity for it returned with full force.

The mirror in the elevator reflected his frown, and almost automatically he took off his narrow-brimmed hat, refusing to lighten his expression. His thin face with its prominent cheekbones and dark eyes, slanted downward at the corners, stared back gloomily. He turned and punched the button marked "4" with unnecessary emphasis. If this didn't pan out, he'd just give up. He was not going to play nursemaid to any out-of-town kid of twenty, even if her grandfather had founded the firm where he worked.

Nick Tyler had never met Simon Sherrill of Buffalo, who had retired as chairman of the board of the Sealtight Siding Corporation several years before Nick became head of the advertising department of the firm. He wished he had never heard of the old gentleman.

The founder of Sealtight regarded his granddaughter, Torre, as the apple of his eye, according to the president of the company. He wanted her to come to New York and work in the company offices, but he also wanted the officers of the firm to keep an eye on her. Torre Sherrill was described as beautiful. Nick's mouth twisted scornfully. In her grandfather's eyes, Torre Sherrill was of course Helen of Troy, Aphrodite and a few of the seraphim. The only thing he didn't claim for her was wings!

The girl who answered his ring gave Nick Tyler a pleasant surprise. She was not too tall, but she carried herself so erectly she appeared taller. And she was not pretty, but she had a clean, wholesome look, a square chin and steady amber eyes.

"Miss Vail?" Nick asked.

The girl at the door kept her hand firmly on the knob. "I am Miss Vail," she admitted. "But the ad distinctly said I wanted two *girls* to share the apartment. . . ."

"Yes, I know." Nick Tyler put on his most ingratiating smile. "And your roommates must be from out of town. I am inquiring for a girl from Buffalo. She hasn't come to town yet, but she has a job with our firm—in my department, in fact. May I come in?"

"Well, yes," the girl agreed hesitantly. "But I don't

see how you can get a place for someone else to live. Maybe she won't like it here."

As Nick walked into the new and sparsely furnished apartment, he made up his mind Torre Sherrill *would* like it here—even if he had to tie her into that hard, atrocious overstuffed chair. This Miss Vail was a no-nonsense type; once Simon Sherrill's granddaughter was ensconced as her roommate, he—Nick—would have done what was required of him, and the girl could like it or not, as she pleased.

Miss Alfreda Vail became noticeably more interested as he explained his dilemma. She did not think it strange that Torre Sherrill's grandfather should be concerned for the girl's welfare in New York; in fact, she approved. She explained her own difficulties in finding a place to live and smiled in a friendly fashion. Nick drew a deep breath of relief; Miss Vail was much more attractive when she smiled, and he had the exhilarated feeling he had won her approval.

"The apartment is small," Miss Vail said deprecatingly, "but I think three working girls will find it comfortable. Let me show you around: the sofa there is a day bed. Then this little hall leads to the bath and to the bedroom proper. This, she said, looking at him anxiously for the first time as she indicated the arch at the end of the bedroom," is really only a dressing room. But as you can see, there is room for a cot. And it's quite comfortable. Sit on it for a minute."

Nick gingerly sidled between the closet and the cot and managed to sit down and bounce experimentally.

"A foam rubber mattress," Alfreda Vail said smugly.

Nick Tyler looked out of the narrow window at the uninspiring view of the court. In his opinion, whoever drew the dressing room cot was getting the short end of the stick. He said, as he followed Miss Vail back to the living room:

"You will take the bedroom, I presume."

She shook her head. "Since we are all going to share the expense, I don't think that would be fair. I thought we would each take turns for one week at a time, so if there is any advantage to sleeping in the bedroom or living room, we'll each have a chance to enjoy it."

Nick Tyler gave a shout of laughter. It was partly an expression of relief at having solved a ticklish problem, but Miss Vail stiffened.

"Pardon me," Nick said, although he was still smiling, "but I can't help thinking what a typically feminine solution to a problem you have worked out. I'm sure Miss Sherrill will like you and will enjoy living here. Now, may I pay you a month's rent in advance? My boss gave me this blank check," he said hastily, "drawn on the company. He'll be pleased to know Mr. Sherrill's granddaughter is so well taken care of."

Alfreda Vail looked as if she were about to protest, but at that moment the doorbell rang and she went to answer it. A tall, statuesque blonde, dressed in a smart suit of lime green with a "fedora" to match, asked in an assured manner:

"Miss Alfreda Vail?" Then, as she looked into the room and saw Nick Tyler unfolding his long, lean frame from the chair by the table, she smiled radiantly and walked in.

"I hope the rent isn't too high," she said with a mocking glance at Nick. "This apartment seems most attractive and well-furnished, including a built-in escort!"

Alfreda Vail blushed and stood tongue-tied with embarrassment, while Nick Tyler looked at the newcomer coldly.

"*You're* not from out of town," he said sharply. "Goodbye, Miss Vail. Miss Sherrill will be here tomorrow evening."

Cindy Lamson came out of the subway and walked north along Lexington Avenue, sniffing the fresh air appreciatively. She hated the subway, particularly the long trip into town from what was almost Albany, in her opinion. But — she glanced again at the folded advertising section of the *Times* in her gloved hand—if she could get to share this apartment in the East Seventies, she need use the subway only occasionally. There were buses; there might even be a taxi now and then. Most important, if she went out on a date—and she had made up her mind there would be many dates in the future—she would not have to confess she lived so far uptown.

This was her year of decision, Cindy Lamson had told herself when she took the job of information clerk at the luxury hotel in New York which had opened its own office for the benefit of guests who wanted to attend the World's Fair. It was part of Cindy's job to look glamorous, gay and super-intelligent about the biggest and most complex Fair ever assembled in one spot at any time anywhere in the world. And she knew she was handling the work well. But she had to get the business of where to live settled before she planned for the future.

The ad had specifically stated there was room for only two to share the apartment; both must be girls from out of town. Well, thought Cindy Lamson, turning east and walking more quickly, she had been born in Penobscot, Maine. It was true she had left at the age of ten months and had been raised in Boston, which she claimed as her birthplace, too, occasionally. But for the last five years she had been working in New York, living in Manhattan when the modeling jobs were lucrative and moving to other boroughs when there was need for economy.

And she was getting old. In the modeling field, twenty-three was pretty well on in years. It was high time she thought of a home and marriage: not as Rad Farnsworth described it: in the modern equivalent of a vine-covered cottage, but as she, Cindy, thought of marriage: exquisite clothes, stunning jewels, frequent trips abroad and an adoring, sophisticated husband to answer every wish of her heart.

This had seemed like pretty big dreaming, even for her, Cindy Lamson admitted to herself, pausing before the building she was to enter. But since she had met Jacques Millet—who did something mysterious and, she was sure, important at the French Consulate—Cindy had felt in her bones that before the World's Fair closed, she would see her dream come true.

Studying herself in the mirror of the elevator, Cindy knew she did not look as if she had arrived in New York yesterday. But, she shrugged, if the girl who had advertised was a new arrival herself, perhaps she would not recognize the patina of sophistication Cindy had worked so hard to achieve.

She pushed the bell, and the door opened almost at once. The girl standing there was plain, shorter than she was and should never have chosen that style of hairdo, or such a gaudy print dress.

"Miss Alfreda Vail?" Cindy asked. She looked into the apartment and, almost without meaning to, walked in. The tall, thin man just getting to his feet was as Ivy League in appearance and manner as his very correct dark suit and shoestring tie. Not stopping to think, Cindy said brightly:

"I hope the rent isn't too high. This apartment seems

most attractive and well-furnished, including a built-in escort!"

She knew from Miss Vail's expression she had said the wrong thing. But the very correct young man needn't have been so quick with his smart retort: "*You're* not from out of town."

Cindy thought fast. She had made a big blunder, but if there was still room for her to live there, she was certainly going to do her best to persuade Miss Vail to let her move in. She needed desperately to move back to Manhattan, and she needed a good address.

Wearily, Alfreda Vail sat on the day bed, then finally stretched out and closed her eyes. It was after two o'clock, and she should be thinking of getting something to eat—a sandwich and a cup of tea—if only to break in the new kitchenette. But at the moment it was heavenly to be alone and to know the question of the apartment and her roommates was settled, at least for the month to come.

It wouldn't have been so frustrating, Alfreda thought, if she had been able, as she planned, to choose her roommates. As it was, she felt *they* had picked *her*. After Cindy Lamson left, promising to move in the next day, there had been five other girls. They were all young, nice-looking and disappointed when they heard the apartment was already rented to others. If she had felt free to choose, Alfreda felt she might have asked one of the other girls to share, instead of Cindy Lamson.

But neither Cindy nor Nick Tyler had left her a choice. She suspected Nick had been glad to solve a troublesome problem involving the granddaughter of the owner of his firm. She knew Cindy had been fearful of being turned down because she had been born and brought up in Boston.

"Boston is really a small town, in a way," Cindy had explained (after carefully finding out that Alfreda had never been there and knew no one who had). "I feel so lost in New York; frightened, really." This described so exactly how Alfreda had felt when she first arrived, she had immediately decided to accept Cindy as a roommate. After all, Cindy couldn't help it if she hadn't been born in Missouri!

There was a sharp knock on the door, and Alfreda gave an involuntary groan and looked at her watch. After three! She rose and went to the door, annoyed at having to turn away another roommate. But it was the superintendent, Sam Waters, who stood there.

"Miss Vail, did you leave the water running in your bathroom?"

"Of course not," Alfreda said indignantly. But Sam, moving fast this time, pushed past her through the living room. He came to a stop in the little hall in front of the bathroom door.

"You did!" he said accusingly, as he reached in and

turned off the faucet in the washbasin. "Got a mop?"

Alfreda numbly went back to the small closet in the kitchenette and brought out the brand-new mop she had bought only the day before. Cindy Lamson had shown a particular interest in the bathroom and had complained bitterly about the lack of pressure in the bathroom of the apartment where she was staying. Alfreda had invited her to test the pressure; Cindy must have put in the plug and then neglected to turn the faucets off completely.

"Never mind, miss," Sam was saying as he worked with the mop. "Them fuss-budgets downstairs got to have something to complain about every day. If it ain't the ceiling falling down, it's the way the people next door play television. If it ain't their sink stopped up, it's the window's stuck. Always somethin' with them. Never you mind."

But Alfreda did mind. She minded very much. It seemed like a bad omen.

Chapter 2

Cindy Lamson leaned back in her chair and patted her stomach. "You'll sure make some man a good wife," she observed, smiling at Alfreda Vail. "In ten days we've been here, this is only the third meal we've had *chez nous,* but each time, by some miracle, you've turned out a gourmet dinner in that tiny kitchenette."

"You're so right, Cindy." Torre Sherrill stretched luxuriously. "I tried a restaurant down near the office last night, and I swear it was like eating sawdust."

Alfreda beamed at them; she was lucky to have two such wonderful roommates, she felt. "I like to cook," she confessed. "If you girls would stay home more, we could really save money eating here, and I don't mind shopping a bit."

"Is that why you came to New York?" Cindy demanded. "To *cook?* Ye gods!—with hundreds of restaurants at the World's Fair and room for almost twenty thousand to eat at one time, you want to shut yourself in this apartment every night and *cook?* You must be off your rocker!"

Alfreda Vail blushed and began to gather up the dishes. "I like to cook," she repeated defiantly. "And I didn't mean to eat home every night. As a matter of fact, Friday night I'm being taken to dinner at the Fair."

"Who's your date?" asked Torre. She felt a little sorry for Alfreda, especially when Cindy Lamson spoke in that patronizing and condescending way.

"He's quite nice. He was born in Kansas City, but he lives in Chicago now. He's going to be at the World's Fair a lot, he tells me."

"Nice-looking?" asked Torre.

"Has he got money?" asked Cindy.

Alfreda laughed at them both. "Yes, Torre, I think he's nice-looking. As for money, Cindy—I don't think that's important."

"It's important," Cindy said grimly. "Just take my word for it. But if you're going to step out, Alfreda, can't you do something about your hair?"

"I should get another permanent. . . ." Alfreda faltered.

"No!" both girls shouted in unison.

Alfreda looked at them in amazement. There was no doubt of their sincerity, and yet they had mentioned getting a new hair style. For the past several years, in Kansas City, that had meant getting a permanent; not a fuzzy one, but something she could set so that it waved back from her forehead. Alfreda had a feeling her explanation of how she meant to arrange her hair would not be acceptable to anyone who looked as smart as Torre or as beautiful as Cindy.

"Suppose you tell me what you mean," she said finally, and listened with astonishment to criticisms of her hair and the way she wore it, of her clothes and her makeup—even of her name.

"But I can't change my name," Alfreda said, making an effort to keep her voice steady. She was perilously close to tears. "I'm named for Father."

"So I gathered," Cindy said dryly. "But there are such things as nicknames; my name is really Cynthia. Don't you have a middle name?"

"It's Myrtle—I was named for a great-aunt. Sometimes people call me Freda," she offered in addition, but Cindy only groaned.

"How about Veda?" Torre said with sudden inspiration. "Veda Vail? Veda—Veda—yes, I like that. Here—" She flicked some water from her glass across the table. "You are now re-christened Veda Vail. And don't object," she warned, "or you'll be sorry. Can you imagine a tall, dark and handsome man trying to say: Alfreda, Alfreda, wilt thou be mine?' No—no, it can't be done! But when the one and only whispers: 'Veda, my sweet— my own darling Veda,' he cay say it with a real throb in his voice."

"All right," said Cindy impatiently, "you've done

your part, Torre. Now leave the creation of Veda Vail, the dazzling maiden who will take New York by storm, to me. That is, if you are willing?"

If she was willing! Did anyone ever have two such kind, sweet, helpful roommates? They were like the sisters she had always longed for, and had never had. Some of the sparkle in her eyes was in her voice as she answered them.

"Veda! It sounds so exciting, Torre. And of course I'll do exactly as you say, Cindy. You're both angels to take so much trouble."

"So what do I do—now that my good deed is done?" Torre demanded. "Do I just sit around and comment?"

"Not at all," Cindy said sweetly. "You can clear the table and wash the dishes."

Some time later Veda stood before the full-length mirror in back of the bathroom door and looked at herself with unbelieving eyes. This was a girl she had never seen before; a girl with all the freshness and open charm of a person born to love the country, overlaid with the sophisticated beauty and glamour of a New York model.

"I'm somebody else," she gasped.

"You're Veda Vail! You're smart, attractive and look as if you'd be nice to know," said Cindy Lamson briskly. "Now go into the living room and show Torre how you look, but remember—that dressing gown belongs to her. I'd better see what I can do about this bathroom—it looks like a disaster area."

But Cindy could not wait to see the effect of the new Veda on Torre. She followed her roommate into the living room, and Torre, who had taken off her dress and was finishing the dishes in her slip, almost dropped the plate she was drying.

"That's a satisfactory reaction," Cindy commented, "but do be careful. Veda is going to have lots of uses for her money besides buying new china. Buying new clothes, for instance."

"Her hair isn't the same color!" Torre said accusingly. "It's like dark honey."

"And the permanent is almost out," Veda said with satisfaction, running her hand lightly over the smoothness on top of her head. "Oh, Cindy! How can I ever thank you??"

"I did do a good job," Cindy admitted smugly. Her own costume consisted of a large bath towel, wrapped around her like a sarong. Her blonde hair was severely pulled back from her face and, since her shoulders were bare and she had not removed her makeup, the effect was that of full evening dress. "Doesn't your housecoat look wonderful on Veda?" she teased Torre. "That off-shade of pink is really hers."

"I rather fancied it on myself," Torre said with mock resentment.

"With your eyes?" Cindy's eyebrows shot up. "Blue

—my dear, but blue. Maybe yellow once in a while."

"All right; I'll sell it to you, Veda," Torre gave in. "But only a dollar less than I paid—I've only worn it twice."

"I have a dress, too, that might be all right," Veda said hesitantly. "It's a print, but there's a lot of pink—" As Cindy shook her head, she added meekly: "But I'll keep my promise and get a new pink suit. Light-weight tweed, you said?"

Cindy nodded absently. Ever since she had grown up, she had had the urge to "make people over"—to make them into the image she saw when she first met them. Veda, with her smooth hair turned up only slightly at the ends, with the odd lift at the corners of her eyes emphasized by the wings of her brows, with that square, forthright chin balanced by a generously lipsticked mouth—Veda was the best creation to date, she thought to herself.

"Thank you, Torre, for cleaning up," Veda said humbly. "And I don't know how to thank you, Cindy, for doing so much for me. It's wonderful to have sisters." She felt silly tears coming to her eyes and blinked hard. "Maybe we ought to have a cup of tea," she began when the doorbell gave a sharp, loud buzz.

"Cindy, did you leave the tap in the bathroom running?" Torre demanded. The blonde looked guilty, but Veda said quickly:

"I turned it off."

"Maybe Reba or Sam is checking up on us; anyway, I'm getting out of here," Cindy said, and made a hasty exit back into the hall.

"Me, too." Torre picked up her dress from the chair and ducked in the same direction.

Both girls would stand there, with the door partially closed, and listen until they were assured all was well. They had all three agreed upon this procedure as being the only sensible one when opening the door to an unknown caller. Veda was pleased to remember this now as she went toward the door. It was good to have two "sisters."

They even had a silly code. If the one answering the door said: "Hello," or greeted the caller by name, the other two would know it was okay and keep out of sight. But if the person was a stranger, or looked dangerous, the person opening the door was to say frigidly:

"Is there something I can do for you?"

They had not decided what was to be done then; since the telephone was in the living room, there would be no chance to phone for help. Torre had once suggested she might open the dressing room window onto the court and shout, but Cindy had told her she would sound awfully silly if it were just a brush salesman.

Veda, however, had no qualms as she went to the door. It was only eight o'clock on a beautiful summer evening. She opened the door wide and froze with her hand on the knob.

He was a big man, and in the narrow apartment house hallway he looked as if he had strayed by mistake from some primeval forest. In one hand he carried a large, square and very narrow overnight case.

"Is there something I can do for you?"

Veda was not even conscious she had used the code words. But at once Cindy dashed to her side, the bath brush clutched menacingly in one hand. Torre, with little to choose from in the way of weapons, picked up the letter opener from the desk and said in a voice that trembled only slightly:

"Don't you dare come in here! Get out—or I'll slit your throat!"

The man laughed suddenly; Cindy turned white. "A maniac!" she whispered. "Shut the door, Veda—quick!"

The man overheard her, and his reaction was instant. He no longer smiled, but his eyes flashed as he pushed the door wider and walked into the living room.

"Oh, no, you don't keep me out!" he said triumphantly. "I've lugged that heavy thing over from Flushing, and I'm going to put it down." Suiting the action to the word, he set the case he was carrying on the floor with a thump that, Veda was sure, would bring another complaint from their downstairs neighbors tomorrow.

It was quite a while before she could straighten out

the affair. It was hard—it even sounded ridiculous—
to explain their code system to Wilbur Holland while
he still stood so defiantly in the middle of the floor.
For, of course, Veda realized she knew the man. He was
a friend of Jack Simmons, who worked in her department at the Right-O! Cereal Company. He had been
in her office two or three times.

Because Wilbur Holland came from Kansas City,
Veda had taken an instinctive liking to him, almost as
though he were "home folks" from 'way back. Jack
Simmons had been vague about what Wil did—"something to do with seeds"—out at the Fair. The last time
she had talked to Wil Holland, Veda remembered, he
had seemed particularly interested in her description of
the apartment and her roommates, but she certainly
had not asked him to stop in.

Cindy, elaborately apologizing for her costume
after the introduction, made a lesiurely exit, waving the
bath brush like a fan. Veda couldn't help but feel
Cindy's emphasis on her becoming déshabillé called the
guest's attention to the satin smoothness of the model's
shoulders. Torre, evidently genuinely embarrassed about
appearing in her slip, simply vanished.

"Say—I'm awfully sorry to come barging in like this,
big oaf that I am," Wilbur Holland apologized. "I
keep forgetting, when I think of you, that I'm not back
home. In this city, I guess you're supposed to phone and
ask if someone wants to see you."

"I'm always glad to see you, Wil," Veda said, trying to make up for her former lack of cordiality. "I didn't know you knew my address. . . ."

"Jack told me," Wil said simply.

"I'm glad he did." Veda tried to ignore the large case standing on the floor. She didn't think that even in Missouri a gentleman came calling on a lady carrying a large suitcase, but maybe Wilbur Holland had other ideas.

"Won't you sit down?" she invited. "The smaller chair is more comfortable, but I think you'd better take the big one."

"Sure; thanks." Wil glanced around the room appreciatively, but he did not sit down. "Nice place you have here but, like you said, it needs warming up. Where will I put this?" He nodded toward the case.

"What is it?" Veda, glad she could at last acknowledge its presence, looked more closely at the case. It seemed very narrow to hold clothes—even one suit.

"It's a portable television," Wil Holland said. "What did you think—Lord! Did you think I was moving in?"

Veda laughed with him. "No, not really. But I had forgotten we talked about our lack of a TV. And I surely didn't expect you to go out and buy one. . . ."

"I didn't buy it," Wil Holland said quickly. "Somebody in the head office back in Kansas City thought we might need one at the Fair exhibit. We already had three. So when you mentioned you didn't have one yet—

I borrowed!"

It was a very generous gesture, Veda thought, and she thanked Wil warmly for the set. There was really only one place for a TV in the room—on top of the desk. That made it necessary to move several chairs, but finally Wil had the TV placed to suit him, and tuned it in. The program came through clearly, and Veda clapped her hands in delight.

"You know, Wil," she said earnestly, "I think New York is just a big, overgrown little town. Everyone I've met is so friendly and helpful. Take Cindy and Torre—they're like the sisters I never had."

"Perhaps," said Wil, turning off the TV, "it's all in the way you approach this town—or any town. If you come expecting coldness and suspicious characters, that is what you find. But if you're a sweet, lovable person who is looking for friends and the New York equivalent of neighbors, you find them, too."

"And you think I am a sweet, lovable person?" Veda asked, smiling at him impishly.

Wil grinned back and caught her arm before she could move away. What would have happened then, she did not get a chance to find out.

"Oh, Veda, will you tell me—sorry! Am I interrupting something?"

Cindy Lamson had come into the room, and now she was dressed in a stunning white piqué sheath that fitted her fragile midriff like a second skin. The single ornament on the dress was a huge white chiffon rose placed at the deep "V" of the décolletage. Her blonde hair was swept high and up—every hair in place.

"You could interrupt anything," Wil Holland assured her, looking at the picture she made as she stood hesitantly in the doorway.

"Thank you, sir." Cindy came into the room with the smooth walk of a trained model. "I bought this only yesterday, and I wanted to ask you, Veda, if you think they did a good job in the fitting?"

Cindy turned around slowly, her eyes never leaving Wil's face, although her words were for her roommate.

"The fit is fine," Veda said, forcing herself to keep her tone pleasant. "I wouldn't take a deep breath, or you might get in trouble. But it's a lovely dress," she added.

Veda felt cheated, almost hollow inside. Cindy Lamson was capable of being supremely unselfish in helping another girl to look her best. But she was also capable of trying to steal the other girl's man!

Chapter 3

"Here's your pass to the Fair. Don't lose it; they're hard to come by."

Torre Sherrill had closed her stenographer's notebook and, after an impersonal: "Will that be all, sir?" was on her feet preparing to go back to her own corner. Now she reached across Nick Tyler's desk and took the pass.

"Thanks," she said. She would have moved away, but Nick waved her back to the chair she had just left.

Torre Sherrill was not the fastest typist in the organization, and her shorthand was not entirely dependable, but she was trying hard—Nick gave her credit for that. As the granddaughter of the founder of the firm, in a job made to order for her, she could have coasted along without raising her hand. But instead, she tried.

In addition to her do-or-die atttiude, Torre Sherrill had further attributes which Nick Tyler admitted made her an acceptable secretary for him. She was tall; her dark hair was smartly cut; she was long-limbed and had a graceful walk that called to mind—Nick's mind, anyway—a young birch tree.

His new secretary also had a firm conviction that what present-day architecture needed were more dedicated women architects. She had explained to Nick that her main objective in coming to New York at this time was to study the buildings at the World's Fair. With this ambition Nick was in complete accord, because he was interested in architecture, too—although he had reservations about women's place in the field.

Now, having resumed her seat as her boss indicated, Torre was looking at him expectantly with eyes which were unusually large and luminously blue, as he had already noted.

"Have you," he began hesitantly, "studied architecture?"

"Oh, yes!" said Torre. "I've read just loads of articles—illustrated, too. I'm simply fascinated by the evolution of architecture in America, all the way from Victorian gingerbread to Frank Lloyd Wright."

"Um," Nick Tyler commented. "Well, architecture in this country didn't start with Victorian gingerbread, you know; it was—you might say—something that grew out of a desire to outdo the neighbors. People who could afford it piled one gimcrack after another on the outside as well as on the inside of their houses."

"You do know a lot about architecture, don't you?" asked Torre admiringly.

"Very little," said Nick. "I'm only trying to learn. But about your idea of studying different styles of architecture at the World's Fair, I think you have something. Perhaps together we could—"

Nick stopped, reluctant to make a suggestion which might sound as if he were taking advantage of his position as head of the department to force his attentions on this girl. Since she was the granddaughter of the company's founder, mightn't it be construed as an effort on his part to build himself up with the old man, rather than as just a friendly gesture?

On the other hand, Torre seemed at once so naïve and so eager about studying architecture, he felt duty bound to help her. Moreover, he had his own career planned, and he was not dependent on the favor of the founder of the Sealtight Siding Corporation to get ahead in the world. Hang it all—he knew he had what it would take to make a name for himself as a designer of buildings!

Nick became aware of Torre's great blue eyes still fixed expectantly on him. She must think the cat had gotten his tongue.

"You're not forgetting we have a date tomorrow to see the Fair?"

"I can hardly wait!" Torre said happily. "I've already told Gander I'm going with you. The minute I get back, I'm going to sit right down and tell him all about those fabulous new buildings."

"You'll write Gander?"

"Grandfather Sherrill. I call him Gander—from the days I couldn't say Grandfather, you know. He's terrifically interested in my ambition to be one of the pioneer women builders of the future."

"Oh!" Nick could think of nothing else to say.

"Maybe I'll take along a sketchbook. Anyway, on some visit to the Fair I promised Gander I'd make rough sketches of the buildings—my impression of them, you know. He'll be so proud. He always wanted to be an architect himself, but he didn't have time, what with building a business instead of a building! But since I like architecture and I'm the only grandchild, Gander is counting on me to make his dreams come true."

Nick stared at her. The girl wasn't vain, he was sure; only honest. It was a kind of honesty he had never met before, and it baffled as well as charmed him.

But—mentally he shook himself—this would never do: the *rapport* he felt for Torre Sherrill must be held carefully in check. He must not become too personally interested in her. After all, he was merely an employee of the Sealtight outfit, and this girl had as good as admitted she was to be her grandfather's heiress. He could assist her in the pursuit of architectural knowledge, but he must at all times maintain the dignified rôle of tutor. Nick managed to repress a sigh.

"There's just one thing," Torre said hesitantly. "When I told Cindy Lamson—one of my roommates— we were going to the Fair, she said she was going, too, with a friend of hers. She asked if we'd have any objections to double-dating. I don't. Do you?"

Nick hoped he did not show that he minded very much. He looked into Torre's pleading eyes and said, not too heartily: "Of course not. The more the merrier." Then he left, without his usual smile.

That night Torre reported to Cindy: "It's all right. Nick is willing to double-date tomorrow."

"What did he say?"

"Just that he didn't mind," Torre reported.

"Not jumping for joy, exactly," Cindy commented. "But Conrad Farnsworth is such a stick, I'd really like another man around to brighten things up."

"Isn't that an odd way to speak of a man you're engaged to?" asked Torre.

"Who said we were engaged? He hasn't given me a ring!"

"Maybe he's noticed you already have an engagement ring or two," said Veda. She came into the room, drying her hair with a towel that all but concealed her face, as well as her head. Veda had seen the engagement rings, but she knew that Cindy didn't regard them with any sentiment. Nor would she discuss them.

"If you're finished with the bathroom," Cindy said now, "I'd like to take a shower." She left the room, ignoring Veda's remark.

Veda didn't care; she wanted to talk to Torre. Toweling her hair vigorously, she finally managed to ask: "If Cindy and her date are going with you, would you mind if Wil Holland and I came along, too? I think it would be fun for Wil to be with a crowd. He doesn't know many people in New York—and I don't, either. Mostly when we have a date, we walk, or go to a museum or some little restaurant he's heard about. I like it, but I suppose it's dull for him. And if we were all together—well, you know—"

Torre smiled at her roommate, understanding how hard it was for Veda to make the request.

"What Nick actually said was: 'The more the merrier,'" she told Veda. "Nick Tyler likes you, Veda, you know that. Otherwise I wouldn't be here. He arranged for me to live in this apartment."

"If you think it's all right—" Veda said, still hesitant. "I'm meeting Wil at noon."

"Nick and I will leave the office about one o'clock and get a sandwich somewhere," said Torre. "Suppose we all meet somewhere at the Fair—at the Unisphere? Let's say three in the afternoon. I think that will be all right with Cindy, too."

"Oh, that's a grand idea—I'm sure we'll have a wonderful time." Veda went back to the dressing room, which was her "pad" for the week, to get her hairbrush. "I'll wear my new pink suit," she said happily.

Torre smiled at her fondly. It was really a pleasure to do things for Veda; she was so grateful for a little attention, and she regarded every occasion as a special treat—like a child let out of school.

Veda and Wil Holland were waiting at the Unisphere when Nick and Torre arrived; almost simultaneously Cindy and Conrad Farnsworth stepped off one of the Fair buses. Cindy's eyes danced as she caught sight of Wil.

"The big seed expert!" she exclaimed. "Just the man I wanted to see. Veda, darling, d'you mind if I ask our 'TV donor' a few questions?" Without waiting for an answer, she slipped her arm through Wil's and chattered on:

"This couple who live in Connecticut stopped at my booth today and wanted information about a rock garden. I had some stuff I could give them, but I should have more information—"

Torre, looking at the patient, humble expression on Conrad Farnsworth's round face, felt sorry for the man and moved to his side. He was shorter than Nick and heavy-set; he seemed the type picked by Fate to play a minor role in life.

"Hi!" said Torre. "Nick and I are taking a walking tour of the Fair this time out. What do you think?"

"Fine," Rad Farnsworth said gratefully. "I love to walk, and we can see so much that way."

"Let's go, then." Torre slipped her hand under Rad's arm and turned toward Nick. Meanwhile Veda, seeing the others all talking together, moved up to Nick and said, laughing:

"I guess we're the leftovers. Shall we console each other?"

"Sure thing!" Nick said heartily. "Follow us!" he said over his shoulder as he took Veda's arm. Torre and Rad followed closely, but it was a few minutes before Wil Holland, seeing them move off, nudged Cindy and they tried to fall in line.

Cindy was slow to notice the others had started off, and there were quite a few strangers separating the party when they finally sauntered on.

"It's a funny thing about rock gardens," Wil Holland was saying quietly. "There are a number of different factors to consider."

"Do I hear calypso music?" interrupted Cindy. "And steel bands?"

"Could be—we're passing the Caribbean Pavilion."

"I hear they have limbo dancers. Let's go in!"

"The others are way ahead now," Wil objected. "We'd better stay with them."

"Do we have to?" asked Cindy, but apparently Wil did not hear her. They were passing the inviting pavilion, and the calypso singers effectively drowned out her words.

"There are gardens and fountains everywhere," Wil said apologetically. "We can't see them all the first time." But Cindy had stopped before a carved wooden gateway leading to an exquisitely designed four-story house. "That's the Republic of China Pavilion," Wil said, consulting his guide book.

"Yes, I know," Cindy murmured. "They serve tea here."

"Yes, I suppose so." Wil looked at her steadily for a moment and then added, "The others have gone on. We mustn't lose them."

Cindy sighed and reluctantly accompanied him past the pavilions of Polynesia, Indonesia and Hong Kong. They caught up with the others just outside the Spanish Pavilion, and they were all together when the sound of electronic bells brought them to a stand-still before the Coca-Cola Pavilion.

Nick Tyler opened up a folder and assumed a lecturer's stance. "The glass-enclosed area at the base of the hundred-and-twenty-foot tower is the console that brings to life the six hundred and ten bells of this carillon, the world's largest,' he read. "Look—you can see the carillonneur in there now."

"What a terrific job he has!" Rad exclaimed.

"The carillon comprises sixty-one notes in chromatic range of different types of bells," Nick informed them.

"Sounds impressive," said Torre, "but I don't know what it means."

"Let's go inside and have a look around," Rad Farnsworth suggested, taking Torre's arm. Nick and Veda followed them, but Cindy, apparently oblivious to the others, drew Wil closer to the base of the tower.

"Isn't it marvelous!" She sighed ecstatically, standing as if fascinated by the spectacle of the celebrated artist who was playing.

Wil stood beside her quietly for a moment and then said: "The others have gone inside. Perhaps we'd better go in, too. We'll lose them if we let them get too much of a head start."

"But that, darling, is the general idea," Cindy said, laughing at him.

Wil Holland did not return her smile. He looked at the beautiful blonde so seriously that her smile gradually faded. "Did I say something wrong?" she asked finally.

"I don't know what Veda told you about me," he said abruptly, "but I imagine she mentioned I used to live in Kansas City?" Cindy nodded, her expression puzzled. "I gather you've never been farther west than New York," Wil said, still in that sharp tone, "so you assume we're still tilling the soil with our bare hands out there."

Cindy continued to stand and look at him, almost as if she could not believe what he was saying.

"You're very beautiful, Cindy Lamson," Wil continued, and his voice was softer. "And you're most attractive to men. But let me give you a little tip. Don't think all men who were raised in the Midwest are country bumpkins and can be led around by the nose. And don't overestimate your own charm. Now, shall we join the others?"

Some time later Rad Farnsworth said to Torre for the fifteenth time: "I wonder where Cindy and Wil are?"

"They'll be along," she said indifferently. "Look, Rad—we're in a forest. See the monkeys and the birds!"

"We're in a tropical forest near an ancient temple of Angkor Vat," said Rad, reading from his guide book. "I believe it's a Cambodian forest."

Next, they found themselves on the promenade deck of a cruise ship at night, riding at anchor off the coast of Rio de Janeiro. Lights twinkled across the water from a distant beach, and Latin music drifted from the ship's lounge.

"I'd like to know how they manage this kind of magic," Rad mused.

"If you know how it works, it isn't magic," Torre said gently. "And I think, Rad, you'll always be wanting something magical in your life. But just enjoy it —don't try to find out why."

"Are you trying to tell me something, Torre? Something about Cindy?"

"Could be," she told him. "But it will keep. Here she comes now, with Wil."

"Let's wait till the others catch up with us before we go on to the New Orleans' Mardi Gras," Veda was saying to Nick. "I'd like for us to keep together more. I can't imagine how Cindy and Wil got so far behind."

"I can imagine how they did," Nick said dryly. "Your little roommate, my dear Veda, is making a play for your boy friend."

"He isn't my boy friend," Veda protested. "And I don't think Cindy is mean. It's just that she's so very beautiful."

"And does she know it!" Nick commented.

Cindy couldn't help but know it, Veda pointed out reasonably. Everyone kept telling her so. But she did think Cindy was making a mistake to be so concerned about marrying for money instead of love. And she sometimes wondered if her sophisticated attitude was not just a pose.

"She mentioned someone in the French consulate, a Jacques Millet," Veda told Nick, "and she looked all starry-eyed and dreamy. But I haven't met him; I don't think Cindy dates him often."

"She wants to marry for money, does she?" Nick asked reflectively. "Tell me, is your friend Wil Holland in the chips?"

Veda looked her surprise. "Oh, no! He told me himself—he's only a salesman."

Nick laughed and squeezed her arm. "You don't

have to worry about losing your boy friend, then. Any time you want him back, just drop the word to your roommate that he's a lowly sales slave. Sometimes even a smooth operator like Cindy Lamson gets her wires crossed."

Chapter 4

Cindy Lamson stood behind the counter in the vast lobby of the hotel, patting the piles of folders set out before her into even neater arrangement. Her working outfit was becoming, she knew: a slim, blue sheath with the Unisphere embroidered in orange on the pocket and an orange-and-blue striped headband. She smiled to herself as she recalled Wil Holland's comment yesterday:

"You're very beautiful, Cindy Lamson."

Of course that other comment he had made about being treated like a country bumpkin—she shrugged. It didn't mean anything; she would be the subdued and chastened maiden when next they met. The important thing was—he had noticed her looks. If she could only be sure Jacques Millet had been equally impressed. He was so handsome, so suave. It was a pity there had been such a crush at the party; if she had had a little more time, or if she had found the apartment a little sooner so that she could have given him her address—

She smiled mechanically at the stout, gray-haired matron who had paused before her polished counter. In a flat, slightly nasal voice she asked:

"Isn't there some place at the Fair where they record births the minute they happen?"

"The births and deaths are recorded every day," Cindy told her. "The Equitable Life Assurance Society has a pavilion where a map shows the births and deaths occurring in the United States day by day. You put on earphones to get the facts about your state."

"I'm from Ohio," the woman confided, "and my daughter's expecting a baby this week."

"Then you tune in Ohio on the earphones, and your daughter's baby will be a statistic when it arrives." She turned from the beaming prospective grandmother to the portly man patiently waiting his turn.

"You've heard there is a pen-pal pavilion? That's right, sir. The Parker Pen Pavilion picks out an overseas pen pal for you when you fill out a card computer. So you're sure to find someone with a matching background and interests like yours. It's quite fascinating, really."

Cindy went back to patting the piles of folders as the portly man turned away, and her mind returned automatically to Wil Holland. He looked substantial. Perhaps not the type she would prefer, but one of those who would have a comfortable fund which he would increase in a comfortable, substantial way. . . .

"Well, I can't hope to compete for your attention with *him*," said a velvety, assured voice with a hint of a laugh behind the words.

"Jacques Millet!" Caught off guard, Cindy could not help blushing and was furious with herself.

The slim, dark young man looking down at her with an amused expression gave her a graceful way out.

"Don't bother to deny you were thinking of someone else," he admonished. "Your face gave you away—and a lovely face it is, too."

"I am an impersonal answering service, sir," Cindy said in mock reproof. "Was there a question you wanted answered?"

"An important question," the dark young man said gravely. "Will you have dinner with me some evening soon? May I call you?"

"That is two questions," Cindy noted, drawing a pad of paper toward her and writing out the phone number. A middle-aged couple was coming toward her, arguing heatedly about something.

"This miserable job of mine at the French Consulate," Jacques Millet was murmuring, "keeps me running back for conferences every other night. But as long as I can get in touch with you—"

"I think you will find this information useful, sir," Cindy said for the benefit of the couple now waiting at the counter. She folded the slip of paper; Jacques

Millet glanced at it and then put it carefully in a thin leather folder which he restored to his jacket pocket.

"Thank you very much, Miss Lamson," he said formally, and Cindy felt her heart thump painfully as he smiled and turned away.

Torre Sherrill put on her old housecoat and folded back the screen which concealed the kitchenette. She hated to eat alone, but tonight there was nothing else to do. Cindy was working the late shift at the hotel, and Veda had gone to the Fair with Wil Holland. Torre unwrapped the cooked sliced ham she had brought home, and the slices of pumpernickel. She located the frying pan after a moment and poured some cooking oil in it. Maybe a hot sandwich would be more appealing than a cold one.

She wished Nick had asked her to have dinner at the Fair. Maybe he was still miffed with her because she had spent some time with Rad Farnsworth, although several days had passed and he had not mentioned their double date, which had turned into a triple. The next time he asked her to the Fair, she resolved, she would not try to include her roommates.

And of course, as her boss, he was most considerate to her in the office. She knew she made mistakes in transcribing the letters, and Nick always called attention to them in an impersonal way. But he had not asked for another date.

Torre lit the gas and put her ham slice on the frying pan. Nick had been out of the office when she left; perhaps he would call and ask her to dinner. Well, in that case she would refuse. She would say she had already eaten. Torre turned up the gas, and the ham began to sputter satisfactorily.

She was trying to locate the butter in the crowded ice-box when the phone rang. Even as she rushed to answer, she knew it would be hard to keep her resolution to refuse Nick a date.

But it wasn't Nick. A man with a velvety voice said: "May I speak with Cindy Lamson, please?"

"She's not in," Torre said, trying to keep the disappointment out of her voice. "I'm her roommate, Torre Sherrill."

"Hello, Miss Sherrill. I'm Jacque Millet, with the French Consulate. Do you know if Cindy will be in soon?"

Oh, dear, Torre thought, Cindy will be wild when she hears she missed a date with you. She said carefully: "I don't expect her before nine-thirty. But you can see her at the hotel. She's working late tonight."

"I wanted to take her out to dinner at the Fair," Jacques Millet said, "but if she's tied up until that late, I guess it will have to be another time. Frankly, I'm starved. Have *you* had dinner, Miss Sherrill?"

"I'm just fixing it—Oooh! The frying pan's on fire. Hold it. . . ." Torre dashed into the kitchenette and turned off the gas; the flames were leaping high as the cooking oil burned. Quickly, she picked up the pan and turned on the cold water as she dropped it in the sink. There was a loud hiss and a cloud of steam, but no more flames.

"Are you there?" she asked breathlessly when she returned to the phone.

"Sure thing." The velvety voice chuckled. "The modified atomic blast I heard was one flaming dinner being doused with water, I presume."

"Yes, it was," Torre admitted, feeling slightly ridiculous. "I guess I turned the gas too high."

"So your dinner's gone up in smoke," Jacques Millet commented. "It was my fault, you know, so you must let me take you to dinner. Can you be ready in twenty minutes?"

"I don't know," Torre began. But after all, why not? Cindy had been quick to annex Wil Holland when they were all at the Fair. And she had burned up her dinner. "On second thought," she said firmly, "I will accept your kind invitation with thanks. I'll wait for you down in the lobby."

She had a momentary pang of doubt when she had to give him the address. Cindy had never told her how well she knew Jacques Millet and apparently had given him only the telephone number. Well, she was commited only to dinner. Torre glanced at her wrist watch and made a dash for the closet.

From her "third" of the rack she picked a fresh white shift of cotton lace with a ruffled neckline and hem. It went well with her black and white striped blazer. Hastily she removed her makeup and applied fresh and then ran a comb through her hair, letting it fly loose. In spite of her haste, it was almost fifteen minutes later when she descended to the lobby.

Sam Waters, his striped cap pushed back on his head, was standing beside the elevator, sniffing.

"Them people in the apartment below you," he said without preamble, "are always thinking of something to complain about. Now it's fire. They said they smelt smoke. Can you smell smoke?"

Torre started guiltily. "This time they're right," she admitted. "I burnt the ham. At least my frying pan caught fire. But I doused it in the sink right away," she assured the superintendent with a bright smile.

But Sam, for once, was not placated. He walked into the elevator, muttering something under his breath, and jabbed the button. He stared stonily at Torre as the door slid shut.

As she crossed the lobby, the glass door opened and a tall, slender young man came in. He smiled with delight when he saw Torre.

"You must be the girl I'm waiting for."

"Could be." Cindy had good taste in men, she reflected. "In fact, I think you are Jacques Millet. You match your voice."

"'And you are Torre Sherrill," he said gravely, "the girl who burnt her dinner."

"The better to eat with you, kind sir." Torre laughed.

His dark eyes twinkled as he steered her through the door and onto the sidewalk, where he flagged a passing taxi. Torre noticed the off-duty sign, even as the taxi swung in to the curb and stopped.

"Where to?" demanded the driver.

"The Fair," said Jacques as he opened the door. The driver flipped the sign up out of sight, and Torre got in.

"So what's in a sign?" she questioned as they started off with a rush.

"Nothing," Jacques explained. "The cabbies pull down the sign so that if you want to go to the wilds of Brooklyn maybe, they don't have to take you. But us—we're going to the Fair."

"'With a hey nonny nonny?" Torre asked.

"And a ho ho ho!" Jacques agreed.

Veda, buttering toast as it popped from the toaster, reached for the kettle as Torre came into the room.

"I've got everything ready," she said, pouring out the water into the cups on the table. "We're late, you know."

"I know," Torre said, biting into a slice of toast. "Good morning, Cindy," she added as the blonde, yawning, came into the living room.

"I'm tired," Cindy said, ignoring the greeting. "I'm going back to bed after I have a cup of coffee."

"Too bad you had to work late. Wil and I had a wonderful time at the Indian Village in the Fair," Veda added, looking pointedly at Cindy.

"We went on the Swiss Sky Ride," Torre said hastily. "Pass the cream, Veda. That coffee is *hot*."

"With Nick?" Cindy languidly spooned instant coffee into the third cup. "Not that it's any of my business," she said hastily as Torre looked at her strangely.

"Yes, it is your business, because it was your date, really. He asked for you, and when he found out you were working, he asked me instead. You see, I was heating a slice of ham, and it burned while I was answering the phone."

Cindy smiled indulgently. "So Rad Farnsworth dated you behind my back. There's a devoted admirer for you!"

"It wasn't Rad," Torre said unhappily. "It was Jacques Millet."

"Jacques Millet!" Cindy repeated. The smile was wiped off her face, and Torre saw her fling up her head in an odd way. It remined Torre of an afternoon spent at the zoo with a zealous high school science teacher. He had pointed out an African adder, one of the most poisonous, which had drawn back its head in the same way as Cindy did now.

"I didn't think you'd mind," Torre said apologetically.

"He said he was hungry, and I hadn't eaten either."

"You didn't think I'd mind," Cindy mocked, and to Torre's ears her voice had the hiss of a snake. "Well, I do mind. And I tell you right now—you keep away from Jacques Millet, or I'll pull out every hair in your head. I'm the jealous type."

"You're making a terrible fuss about nothing," Torre said, finishing her coffee and picking up her handbag. "Jac and I went to dinner and then on the Swiss Sky Ride; it was all perfectly innocent."

Veda picked up her own handbag and went to the door. "Come on, Torre," she urged. "We've both got to run. Don't be so dramatic, Cindy. One dinner date won't ruin your romance."

"You bet it won't!" Cindy agreed. "But go on to work, both of you. And maybe I won't be here when you get back, Miss Turn-the-other-cheek Veda! Take my advice and get rid of your man-snatching roommate, or you'll wind up going back to Kansas City and life with Papa."

"If you go back to bed, maybe you'll wake up in a better humor," Veda said, pushing Torre ahead of her and closing the door.

"I'm sorry Cindy got so upset," Torre apologized as they went to the elevator. "But I don't think you'll have any trouble finding another girl to share."

"Cindy will stay," Veda said with conviction. "She flares up, but when it's all over, she doesn't hold a grudge. You know, I'm anxious to meet this Jacques Millet myself. He must be quite a person, to have two girls fighting over him before breakfast!"

Nick brushed aside Torre's apologies as she came into the office. He had to hand it to her, he thought as she quickly opened her desk and came over with pencil and notebook in less than a minute. She never traded on her grandfather's position—or ownership—of the Sealtight Siding Corporation.

"I've gone through the mail," Nick said as she sat down beside his desk. Her eyes, he thought, looked particularly large and blue this morning, but he resolutely glanced away from her. "I've decided I'll dictate straight through until we're finished, and then you can type until lunch."

Torre eyed the pile of letters in front of him. "I'll never be able to answer them all by lunch time," she said honestly.

"After lunch, I need you at the Fair. I'm going to look over the construction of the underground house. I hear they have some radically new ideas in the structure. And bring your notebook."

His secretary set her lips in the do-or-die expression Nick knew so well. "In that case," she said, "you'd better start on the dictation, and I'll do the letters as fast as I can."

"Now don't hurry," Nick said at once. "Tomorrow's

another day. We'll get the correspondence lined up, but you needn't rush with the typing."

His secretary looked at him gratefully as he picked up the first letter, and Nick felt guilty. He was not being kind when he asked her to take her time. He was simply appalled at the thought of what Torre, who often made a mishmash of letters she had the whole day to transcribe, might do to his correspondence if she tried to rush the work.

Chapter 5

On the way to the Fair in Nick's car, Torre stole a glance at his rugged profile. He was a handsome man, but somehow he never seemed to relax, at least with her.

"The Underground World Home," she mused. "It's really an old, old idea, isn't it? Sort of like going back to cave-man days?"

"Only this home doesn't need a cave to start with," explained Nick. "I understand it's about five feet underground and contained in a shell of concrete."

"Something suited to the Atomic Age, I suppose," Torre said lightly, hoping for a smile. "I'm afraid the field of architecture is getting more complicated by the minute."

"It is, you know," Nick said gravely, "like everything else."

Torre sighed. The situation she found herself in—dating the boss—was foreign to her experience. Last night, at the Fair with Jacques Millet, everything had been fun. They had talked nonsense some of the time, and had argued about various types of sports—Jac, for instance, thought skiing a waste of time, and she loved it—and it all added up to a fine evening. Today, perhaps because she was conscious of her notebook and pencil, she had a feeling even the glamorous background of the Fair would not loosen the constraint she felt.

The Underground Home proved far larger than she had anticipated: there were nine rooms and two terraces. There were also a fountain and a lily pool and growing plants on the terraces.

"You really don't miss the outdoors in a house like this," Torre said, busily taking notes.

"You're missing the whole concept of this home," Nick said almost angrily. "You can't judge it by regular standards, such as a home wtih a yard and lawn and trees."

Torre felt as if she had been slapped but, she reminded herself, he was her boss. "You mean I should think of it primarily from the protective angle?" she asked. Then she answered herself, "I don't know, Nick. I believe every woman has an instinct for homemaking. She has a sort of dream home in her mind, and while the home will protect her, she thinks of it first as a background for love and marriage and a family."

Nick looked at her sharply but not, she admitted to herself, as if he were the boss. "Would *you* like to live in a house like this, if you and the man you were going to marry planned your future here and he helped you find the right furniture and stuff like that?"

Torre thought for a second and then said slowly: "I wouldn't want to force my ideas on the man I marry. I am interested in architecture, in the actual structure of the house and its layout. If the man I was going to marry was interested in architecture, too, and had similar tastes, then I think I would like to live here. Yes."

Nick seemed to brighten at this, and Torre was glad she had found the right thing to say. He suggested that she put away her notebook and pencil and that they go upstairs and stroll around. Torre meekly did as she was told and followed him to a small park-like oasis where there were benches for the Fair visitors. It was a cloudy, gray day with a slight breeze; Torre was glad to be out in the fresh air, even lacking sunshine, but she did not think it was the moment to say so.

"Speaking of marriage," Nick said abruptly, "I think you're right. Two people who have the same ideas are the best bet for a successful marriage. I mean, if one has forward-looking ideas, the other ought to be more or less of the same mind."

"Other things being equal," Torre added cautiously, wondering where this conversation was leading.

"Meaning money, I suppose," Nick surprised her by saying.

"You sound like Cindy Lamson," she protested. "Only she doesn't want the money to be equal; she wants the man to have the money—lots of it."

"You've got to admit a man with only his salary is nothing better than a fortune-hunter if he marries an heiress."

"I was talking about equal points of view, not money. Yet two people of exactly the same disposition and tastes would surely not make an exciting combination. I think there should be definite differences in temperament."

To herself Torre thought of Jac Millet and how differently they thought on many subjects, yet how wonderfully well they got along.

Nick scowled; he seemed to have lost interest in the subject. Torre was tempted to abandon it, too, but he was the boss and she owed it to him at least to try to keep the conversational ball rolling.

"I suppose I'm prejudiced," she explained, "but it's because my parents had such an ideal marriage. My mother loved fun and giving parties and traveling; my father was big and serious and liked all kinds of sports —and his work. I've heard them argue, often, but there were no bitter arguments. They never quarreled. When the plane they were in crashed, I thought I had lost everything."

"You poor kid." Nick patted her hand and smiled. "I've been wondering about your name. Was 'Torre' your mother's name?"

She shook her head. What had possessed her to talk about her mother and father? She always choked up.

"I'm named for a little Italian village where my mother and father once vacationed," she said, "just before I was born. It's a little fishing village. They were so happy there, they named me after it."

Nick was silent again, and after a few minutes Torre suggested they walk around awhile. They paced along among crowds that seemed enthusiastic, or complaining, or anxious to get somewhere else, but that were at least doing *something,* Torre thought resentfully. She and Nick were ambling along as if they were walking down a dull and uninteresting street.

"We're not far from the Festival of Gas Pavilion," she said finally. "Cindy says they have a dishmaker there that sounds exciting."

"You mean a dishwasher?"

"No. A dish*maker*. You push buttons, and disposable plastic dishes jump out."

"Oh!"

Torre tried again. "Or we could go over to Johnson's Wax—they give you a free shoeshine and hints on how to take care of your car."

Nick stopped her with a hand on her arm and pointed down at his shoes. They were brown suede loafers.

Torre felt herself becoming annoyed. If Nick Tyler wanted to sulk, she thought stormily, they might as well leave the Fair. As if he felt her resentment, Nick said:

"It's getting late. Maybe we should have something to eat."

Instantly Torre tried to meet him halfway. "We could have dinner at the House of Japan," she suggested. "Cindy told me about something called tempura—made of shrimps and vegetables—sort of a pancake. They also give a lesson in flower arrangement." She broke off at Nick's cold expression.

"If you want to go there," he said flatly.

Torre had had enough. In the mood Nick was in, dinner with a rajah would not arouse his enthusiasm. But he was her boss, so she said with false brightness:

"Actually, I'm not the least bit hungry. And I'm a little tired; we did quite a bit of walking. Why don't we call it a day, and when we get back to Manhattan you can drop me at the east side subway entrance? No use to buck uptown traffic."

Nick agreed with alacrity to her suggestion to leave. She made no further attempt at conversation, and Nick concentrated on his driving. Job or no, Torre fumed, if he actually let her off at a subway entrance, she'd never speak to him again. Socially, that is.

To her intense annoyance, Nick did drive up to the subway entrance and, after the briefest of farewells, shot on with the traffic. Torre stood looking after him with disgust.

It served her right for going out with her boss. Jac Millet, with his polished manners and sophisticated charm, would never, but never, act like such a boor!

Veda Vail was thoughtful as she left the offices of the Right-O! Cereal Company. She didn't like the idea of Torre and Cindy quarreling. Even if they agreed to a truce, if they continued to bicker, they lived in such close quarters life would be uncomfortable. As the holder of the lease, she, Veda, would have to choose between asking Cindy or Torre to leave, unless she could figure out a way by which they could both save face.

She knew Cindy Lamson would not for a minute carry out her threat and leave at once. But she would not be at home, either. She might not work as late as she had the night before, but it would probably be after six when she got back. Torre had called and said she would be at the Fair all afternoon; she would also be in late, perhaps later than Cindy.

Veda stopped and bought a small barbecued chicken for herself and had it split in half. If either of her roommates showed up, they could eat together. If not, she would leave the other half in the icebox. She picked up a box of frozen broccoli in the supermarket and some French rolls she could heat. Veda loved the supermarkets in New York; in fact, she loved New York.

She had written to her father, telling him all about the apartment and her roommates; she knew he was pleased to hear she was happy. Which brought her right back to the present problem. What could she do to smooth over the situation between Torre and Cindy?

Veda could understand both points of view. Cindy had tried to latch onto Wil Holland, even though Rad Farnsworth, her own date, had been right there. If Veda had wanted to make an issue of it, she could have become annoyed at Cindy, as Cindy was now annoyed with Torre. But she thought she understood the blonde model.

Somewhere, sometime, she had read that we are most intolerant of faults in others which we ourselves possess. The person who was always late, Veda remembered, became furious if someone else kept him waiting even a minute. It was like that with Cindy. She thought nothing of taking another girl's man, even though she might not be too interested in him. But she was ready to fight like a tiger if someone did the same thing to her.

Veda let herself into the empty apartment and put her bundles down in the kitchenette. It was a problem she did not know how to solve. Meanwhile, she would get dinner. She was tying on a most decorative apron —Cindy's "moving in" gift—when the door opened and Torre came in.

"I'm so glad I don't have to eat alone," Veda said happily, turning on the small oven. "I thought you and Nick would eat at the Fair."

"Let me get into a housecoat, and I'll tell you all about my afternoon with the boss," Torre said grimly. "I'm so mad I could holler and scream."

When she actually started to tell Veda about it, however, the afternoon did not seem so bad. And when Veda suggested perhaps Nick had been preoccupied with another problem, Torre agreed it might be so.

"I'm in no mood to be sweet to Cindy, however," Torre said firmly. "I had a date with Jacques Millet, I enjoyed it, and she's not going to make me out a criminal because I didn't turn him down."

"Well, let's eat," Veda said soothingly. "Maybe Cindy will have forgotten all about it by the time she comes home."

Torre switched off the light in the kitchenette and lit the candles on the table; Veda found a radio program of dinner music, and the two girls smiled at each other happily and toasted each other in tomato juice before they attacked the delicious chicken dinner Veda had prepared.

By common consent they avoided the subject of dates; Veda told of her life in Kansas City while Torre spoke of her adventures at boarding school and her vacations at her grandfather's big house in Buffalo.

"You've lived like a princess," Veda commented, but she was not envious. "I imagine you could have been a debutante and spent your time in charitable endeavors until you married. In fact, I wonder you were allowed to take a job and come here to New York alone."

"My Gander—grandfather to you—is the most wonderful person who ever lived," Torre assured her. "I know he loves me, but he's not possessive about it.

When I told him I wanted a career, he thought of ways to help me. But from here on in, I'm on my own."

They cleared off the table in a leisurely fashion and turned on the TV Wil Holland had brought over. They were still watching an amusing program, with only one dim light in the corner of the living room, when Cindy came in. Veda was thankful for the semi-darkness and wondered if her roommates did not feel the same way.

"Good evening, Cindy," Veda said, determined to clear up the misunderstanding between the girls. "Are you hungry? Can I make you a sandwich?"

"No, thanks. I ate." Cindy was laconic, but her voice was pleasant. "Am I bushed!" She threw herself down on the day bed and, since the commercial was on, continued: "There are some days when I think everyone in the world is stupid."

"Except you?" Torre asked.

It was not said maliciously, but Veda held her breath.

"I'm the stupidest one of all," Cindy said with a rueful laugh. "I'm the one who has to answer their questions."

Veda laughed, too—with relief. It was going to be all right. She was about to make some comment when there was a knock on the door. "It's me," the superintendent's wife called. "Could I see you a minute, Miss Vail?"

"Here we go again," said Cindy under her breath. Veda switched on the table lamp and opened the door.

Reba Waters stood there, an unhappy but resolute expression on her plump face.

"Sam wants me to tell you the people downstairs complained the ceiling of their bathroom is sopping wet and is going to fall down," she said without pre-amble.

Cindy sat up. "Does a day pass when the people downstairs don't complain?" she asked. "Maybe there's a leak in the plumbing."

This was a slur on her husband which Reba Waters would not stand for. "You was the last one out today," she said, accusing the blonde directly. "Sam had to use his key to get in, and he found you'd left the bathroom basin running again. This is the fourth time it's happened, Miss Vail. My Sam has got better things to do. . . ."

"Your Sam should have gotten busy and fixed that blasted ceiling before it fell!"

Veda saw the short, chunky man open the "Exit" door to the stairs and advance on them in a menacing fashion. He was wrapped in a red and white striped bathrobe, and his thick black hair was decorated with a blob of white plaster that looked rather rakish above his unshaved and scowling face. There was no doubt about it: he was the man downstairs.

Reba Waters cringed as he advanced, and Veda said quickly:

"Oh, I'm so sorry. Are you hurt?"

"Of course I'm hurt!" the man howled. "How would you like to have a chunk of wet plaster fall on your head? I'm going to sue—that's what I'll do. If you can't remember to turn off the water when you go out, you girls ought to live in an institution!"

Torre, who had been sitting quietly near the TV, rose and turned it off. Then she came and stood beside Veda.

"You want to sue?" Torre asked pleasantly. "Then I would suggest you call a lawyer and have him present the papers in a proper fashion. I don't think *my* lawyer will like it if I tell him you came up here in that ridiculous bathrobe," the man clutched the garment about him more tightly, "and tried to intimidate defenseless women. My name is Torre Sherrill," she added in the same lofty tone, "and my attorneys are in Buffalo. I'll be happy to give you the address."

The man seemed to wilt, and there was no doubt he felt in the wrong. He was staring at Torre, and he said at last in a voice that quavered:

"Sherrill? You wouldn't be any relation to Si Sherrill, would you?"

"Simon Sherrill of Buffalo is my grandfather," Torre said crisply. "Now if you'll give me your name—"

"Old Si Sherrill's granddaughter!" the man broke in. "He gave me a job years back when I was younger than you, and broke. I can't believe it! His granddaughter living in the same house!"

"And forgetting to turn off the faucets," Torre said

with a warning glance at her roommates.

"Aw, that was nothing. We're all forgetful some-times," the man said abjectly. "Don't mention this to Si—your grandfather, miss. Just tell him Slim was askin' for him—Slim Johnson. He'll remember. I used to be thinner," he said with a nervous laugh, "in those days. Come downstairs, Reba, and help my wife clean up."

When they were gone, there was silence, while Veda, Torre and Cindy stared at each other. Then Cindy, with a wide smile, crossed the room and threw her arms around Torre.

"My own true friend! My pal! My friend in court!" she said, giggling and rocking back and forth in glee. "You are an accomplished liar, and I love you for it."

"It was nothing." Torre grinned. "What's a room-mate for, if not to take the rap once in a while?"

"You can take my dates once in a while, too," Cindy said generously.

Veda smiled at them both. Everything was once more right with her world.

Chapter 6

The offices of the Right-O! Cereal Company were on the seventeenth floor of a modern structure on the Avenue of the Americas. The outside walls were mainly glass, and the effect from inside was almost like that of a tree-house, perched high in the air in a forest of skyscrapers.

Veda Vail had two offices in one corner. Her own was the smaller and uncluttered. The second office held the many files and two skilled file clerks and secretaries who could produce correlated data on available warehouse space, volume of business, packaging costs and other valuable information at a moment's notice. Veda's position as chief statistician for the company was an important one, and undoubtedly she was in an ideal spot to take part in office politics.

The idea never occurred to her. To Veda, her job was, in a way, a type of housekeeping. The reports came in from the five branch offices and were duly noted and filed under various categories. If there was a delay in a report, or one missing, she knew it as surely as a housewife might know she had used the last of her sugar or needed a fresh can of baking powder. Then it was Veda's responsibility to get the information and file it correctly, almost as if she had to go to the store and replenish her pantry.

Veda had little contact with the officers of the company and had only a vague idea of what they did. The one exception was Jack Simmons, a thin, sandy-haired man of indeterminate age, whose title was Vice-President in Charge of Sales. Simmons usually made his requests for information in person, although his dry, un-inflected voice was as impersonal as a weather report. He had brought Wil Holland into the office to show him how efficiently the department of information was managed. That visit had been impersonal, too.

Yet this morning Veda, automatically going through the mail and marking it for filing, knew her relationship with Wil Holland was intensely personal. She had liked him the minute she saw him, looking so big and outdoorsy in her small office, and she knew that he had liked her at once. When she found he had been born in Kansas City and when he had brought a TV set over to the apartment, it had been like one neighbor meeting and helping another if they met in a strange town.

But since she and Wil joined Cindy and Torre and their dates at the Fair, there had been a subtle change in the way Veda felt toward him. She admired the poise of her roommates and the way they managed their dates.

Liking a man when you first met him and letting him know you admired him frankly and openly did not seem the right thing to do.

Torre, for instance, dated her boss, Nick Tyler. She had no hesitation about going with him, yet she didn't appear to like him very well, and she had certainly not enjoyed her last visit to the Fair. Veda could not imagine having a good time with Jack Simmons, either. But then she would not have gone to the Fair with him in the first place!

It was also puzzling to Veda that Torre had casually accepted a dinner invitation from Jacques Millet—over the phone! And on this date she had had fun, apparently without realizing she was only a substitute for her blonde roommate.

Veda took some papers into the next office and gave them to a redheaded file clerk. There was no need for instruction; the girl knew her job. She returned to her desk and sat idle for a moment, thinking of Cindy Lamson.

Cindy openly flaunted two engagement rings; collecting them seemed to be a hobby with her. Her relationship with Conrad Farnsworth, who obviously adored her, was equally casual. If she needed an escort, Rad was only too happy to be with her. She treated him with scorn, yet he apparently made no protest and was content with only an occasional kind word.

Cindy's attitude toward marrying for money was

hard for Veda to understand, too. One night when she came home from work the blonde had described a man she had met that day as a "a big shot exhibitor at the Fair. Loads of money."

"Money isn't the most important thing in the world," Veda had protested.

"To me it is," Cindy had snapped, and seemed all at once much older and worldly-wise. "That's what I'm looking for—a man with money," Cindy had continued. "It's as easy to marry a man with a million as to marry one without even a checking account."

Veda felt a little sorry for her roommate; she must be missing something wonderful when she put so much emphasis on the materialistic side of life. And it had left its imprint on her; Nick Tyler had understood it perfectly when he asked Veda, at the Fair, if Wil Holland was "in the chips."

She herself had never thought about it. She had assumed Wil Holland was a salesman for the seed firm which had an exhibit at the Fair, and that is what she had told Nick Tyler. But, Veda admitted to herself, she did not know, and although she had seen Wil alone, she had found the Indian Village so fascinating she had not inquired about Wil's work.

But lately she had been wondering. There was no reason she should not ask him exactly what his position with the seed company was. Whatever his answer, it would make no difference to her.

Resolutely Veda picked up her work folder and at the same minute the phone rang. Wil Holland's voice was familiar, although he had called her at the office only once before.

"I've been out of town," he said apologetically. "Did you miss me?"

Ordinarily Veda would have admitted she had missed him. But thinking about her two poised and competent roommates, she shifted to a noncommittal:

"We've been so very busy here at the office—" Then, striving for a degree of truth, she added: "I haven't been to the Fair since we were out there together."

"Good," Wil said exuberantly. "For a minute, I was afraid you were going to tell me you'd found another date. How about having dinner with me out there in Flushing tonight?"

"I'd love to," said Veda with her normal enthusiasm, and then wondered if she had sounded too aggressive.

"Any particular spot?"

"Oh, yes—I want to go to the Pavilion of the Republic of Guinea," Veda said promptly.

There was a second of silence on the other end of the phone. Then Wil said thoughtfully: "The Pavilion of the Republic of Guinea? Are you interested in the native food?"

Veda, who had remembered Cindy mentioning the exhibit, could not recall whether or not she had said anything about the food.

"I don't know what the native food of Guinea is," she admitted, "and I don't really care. But the Republic has a ballet troupe. I understand it's frightfully exotic." Again she was quoting Cindy; she would never have chosen the exhibit by herself.

"I'm not up on ballet," Wil said dubiously, "but if that's where you want to go, it's fine with me. I'll pick you up at five-thirty."

Veda sat staring at the phone for several minutes after she had hung up. She had never before taken the initiative with a man who asked her out on a date. But even if she was not so poised as Torre or Cindy, she could at least pretend to be.

The Pavilion of Guinea, Veda discovered when she and Wil arrived there that evening, consisted of three structures: a main building and two small huts which were replicas of the traditional types of buildings found in that country. All three were surrounded by a moat; they crossed the bridge over it to reach the small "island." Veda glanced up at the small huts.

"Thatched roofing," she observed.

"Simulated," corrected Wil.

They glanced inside the huts as they passed; native craftsmen were working on articles which were to be sold at a booth nearby. Wil looked down at her and grinned.

"Are you thinking the same thing I am?" he asked.

"I'm thinking the concentration of a true craftsman is the same in every country, for every art."

"Yes," Wil agreed. "I guess that's why a World's Fair is so important; it makes you realize simple truths."

The main building was circular with a somewhat conical roof—rippled along the edge—set on an open-work steel frame.

"A lacework building with a hat on," Veda commented as they stepped inside.

The ceiling was of woven straw in many colors, which Cindy had told her was exactly like the one in the new house where the President of Guinea lived. Veda thought it a lovely room; the tables were placed around a stage set in the center, presumably where the ballet was presented.

"It doesn't look particularly native or foreign," Veda commented. "It just looks modern, like our 'theater in the round.'"

"I'll try to get a table near the stage," said Wil, "so you can have a good view of the dancers."

But it was evidently a popular spot; every table seemed to be taken. The headwaiter explained that they could either wait a few minutes for a table for two, or share a table. There was one couple who would be leaving soon. . . .

When Veda nodded, Wil told the head waiter to lead the way through the narrow space between tables to one on the other side of the stage. Then the headwaiter stepped aside, and Veda stood staring in amazement at Cindy, her roommate, and the tall, dark, attractive man who was sharing her table.

"How did you track us down?" Cindy asked in a cool tone. It was evident their arrival was far from welcome. Cindy's escort jumped to his feet, and Wil looked at him with a reserved expression.

"It's a small world, to coin a phrase," he said to Cindy. "May we sit down?"

"Please do." The young man pulled out a chair for Veda with a flourish, and Cindy finally said, "Veda darling, this is Jacques Millet; my roommate, Veda Vail. And, Jac, this is Wil Holland." The men shook hands, and then Wil sat down and picked up a menu. He looked up after a second with a baffled expression.

"It's all Greek to me," he admitted, and they laughed.

"Traditional Guinea; not Greek," giggled Cindy. "Tastes divine, though." The words were vague enough, but the blonde's tone managed to make them sound intimate—for Wil Holland alone.

Veda stiffened. Then she smiled and turned to Jac Millet.

"Have you been long in this country?" she asked.

"I was born here," said Jac, and Veda was embarrassed. She was no good at verbal fencing.

"You seem so Parisian," she stammered.

"He works for the Fenrch Consulate," Cindy said in a bored tone. "Well, Jac, shall we get moving? You'll like the ballet, Veda; at least we enjoyed it. But Jac and I have places to go and things to do."

As Wil stood up, Veda had a sudden sinking sensation that he was going to leave her sitting there alone. Cindy was a siren who could lure anyone away. But Wil only put a hand on Jac's arm.

"Before you go, what did you people have to eat?"

Jac smiled and pointed out several items. Wil nodded, and then Jac, with an *"au revoir"* to Veda, followed Cindy. They were soon lost in the crowd.

"Cindy Lamson is surely a beautiful girl," Wil said, turning to Veda with a smile.

"Yes, she is." Veda felt ready to cry. She wished she had never heard of the Pavilion of the Republic of Guinea.

"What's the matter?" Wil asked. "Don't you like your roommate?"

"Of course I do," Veda said crossly. "I don't approve of her attitude toward life, but I suppose it's her business. She told me once that she thought it was as easy to marry a millionaire as a pauper. She's been engaged twice—she has the engagement rings to prove it—but she said an engagement has nothing to do with marriage!"

"You sound rather outraged," Wil said with a quizzical smile. "But then I guess you're an incurable romanticist. Maybe it's because you were born in Kansas City," he teased.

Veda refused to smile. "Then you approve of the mercenary approach to marriage?" she demanded.

"Let's say I approve of Cindy Lamson taking a realistic view of life. She has beauty, youth and intelligence. Naturally she can afford to be choosy."

Veda decided it was time for a little plain talking.

"You remember our visit to the Fair when Cindy took you off on a tour of your own?"

"You were with Nick Tyler," Wil pointed out. He had stopped smiling.

"Yes." Veda bit off the words. "And he told me that I didn't need to worry about my boy—my date—because Cindy Lamson would lose interest in you the minute she found out you were nothing but a salesman."

"Who told Nick I was 'nothing but a salesman'?" Wil asked.

Veda felt the color flood her face, but she determined to talk this out, since she had gone so far.

"I did. Aren't you a seed salesman?"

Wil shook his head. "I'm not. They are probably a very fine group of men, but I'm not a seed salesman. I am a soil engineer; that's why I know Jack Simmons so well."

"But the exhibit, here at the Fair—"

"A subsidiary company. I started to prove some of my theories, but it's now very successful on its own. In fact, there are several companies I own or control, and many others, like the Right-O! Cereal Company, who engaged me as a consultant."

Veda felt sick with humiliation. In attempting to get back at Cindy, she had succeeded only in making herself look like a fool. She picked up a menu and studied it, but she could not see the print clearly—it was all blurred.

"You *own* the seed company and others," she said in a choked voice. "You must have a lot of money."

"Yes," Wil said, his voice grim. "Cindy was right. I'm a good prospect for a gold-digger. But I didn't think *you* were the type!"

Chapter 7

Veda said good night to Wil Holland at the door and came through the lobby with only one thought in mind—to get upstairs and into the private haven of the apartment and cry as she wanted to.

For the past three hours she had held it back. Wil had helped. He had apologized instantly for comparing her with Cindy, and they had both made a pretence of forgetting what had been said for the rest of the evening. The ballet was enjoyable; the food was good. And it was pleasant to stroll around the Fair afterward until Veda thought it was admissable to mention she was tired and suggested that they go home.

But now she wanted to let go, to let all the pent-up emotion and humiliation she felt burst out in tears and sobs. If her roommates were already in, she would lock herself in the bathroom until the storm was spent.

Reba Waters came rushing over to her as she was about to step into the elevator. She was carrying a small, square package which she held out to Veda.

"This came for Miss Lamson this afternoon, Miss Vail. But she isn't home, and your other friend ain't in, either. I don't like to leave it layin' around in the hall. . . ."

"I'll take care of it, Reba."

She knew the superintendent's wife was looking at her closely, but she didn't care. The apartment was empty; she could be miserable in peace!

It was almost an hour later when Torre came in, explaining she had gone to the movies with one of the girls in the office. By that time, Veda had cried her heart out and then had held cold washcloths against her face until the skin felt frozen. After she had undressed and taken a shower, she felt better, if completely spent, but she knew the traces of tears were quite evident. Since it was her week for the day bed in the living room, she would have to face her roommate's questions. But Torre made it easy.

"Did you have a good time at the Fair—holy cow! What happened to your face—as if I didn't know! Never you mind, Veda." She unexpectedly put her arms around Veda and held her tight for a minute. "I had my dose of homesickness last week."

"Thanks, Torre," Veda said gratefully, "that was it—a bout of homesickness. I'll be all right now."

"Good girl," Torre said absently. "The 'Fair Cindy' isn't in yet, I take it?"

"Not yet. There's a package for her."

"Good. I'll stake my claim to the bathroom, then."

Veda called after her: "Would you like some iced cocoa? I'm going to make some."

"Make a lot," Torre called cheerfully. "I could go for a sandwich, too."

Veda felt a lot better once she started fixing a snack. There was a hunk of cheese in the icebox, and a package of English muffins in the vegetable bin where they kept the bread. She decided on cheese dreams and lit the broiler to let the oven heat up while she made the cocoa and got out the ice cubes. By the time everything was ready, Torre came back into the room in her shortie pajamas, and Cindy opened the door.

The blonde model had apparently had a good evening. She was humming a gay dance tune, although she broke off at sight of Veda.

"Why the blues?" she demanded.

"Just homesick," Torre ssaid hastily. "Leave her alone."

"What do you mean, homesick?" Cindy asked in astonishment.

"All out-of-towners get homesick once in a while," Torre said with emphasis. "Don't you ever long to see old Boston once more?"

"Oh, yes. Yes, of course I get homesick!" Cindy said hastily. "Is that package for me?"

"It is. But bring it over to the table and open it. The cheese dreams are ready," Veda said, putting them on the table.

The two girls bit into their muffins and sipped their iced cocoa slowly while Cindy, after one hasty gulp, worked on opening the package. Veda finally handed her the paring knife from the kitchenette, and out of the crushed paper inside Cindy pulled a small green replica of a prehistoric monster.

"Well, what do you know?" the model said, holding it on the palm of her hand. "Rad Farnsworth has a sense of humor after all! He's been out in Chicago for the last few days, but he's been thinking of me all the time while—"

"While you date other men," said Torre, finishing her muffin and licking her fingers.

"He's an awfully cute dinosaur," Veda said, reaching over and examining him closely. "It looks exactly like a miniature of the monsters in the Ford exhibit at the Fair; you know, the ones Walt Disney dreamed up."

Cindy stared at Torre a moment, and then apparently decided to forget it. "What shall I name my baby?" she asked, taking it back.

"Dino, naturally," Torre said at once.

"Dino!" Cindy echoed, nodding. "Thanks, dear. You know all the answers, don't you?"

Torre, although she felt relaxed, did not immediately fall asleep. It was her turn to have the "pad" in the dressing room, and she found it just as comfortable as the bed and liked it better than the day bed in the living room. Anyway, she did not mind lying there quietly, looking out at the narrow bit of sky visible through the window on the court. She liked to think about Nick Tyler and how, after that unfortunate time they had at the Fair, things had worked out so well.

She had typed up her notes on the Underground House, and then she had stayed one evening and sketched her impressions of it. She had worked hastily, depending on a line here, and a little heavier shading there, to convey what the house meant to her. Then she had left her sketches on the desk, intending to mail them to Gander the next morning.

But Nick was standing, looking at the four of them, when she came in. Torre said, a little embarrassed:

"I did them very fast. Something to show Gander."

"I like them. They're fine." Nick looked at her and then smiled slowly. "I was afraid you didn't have a very good time that afternoon, but these look as if you got something out of our visit after all."

"But of course I did." Torre's heart was singing.

"I made some sketches, too. No, I'm not going to show them to you. It's only part of a general idea I have—one I'll tell you about sometime."

It was a nice feeling to be once again on the old footing—not too efficient secretary and indulgent boss. Torre smiled into the darkness. Altogether life was very pleasant, even though there was an occasional bit of bickering with Cindy. She listened now as Cindy, having gotten into bed, suddenly switched on the light and went back into the bathroom. For once, she had remembered to turn the faucet off tight. Veda had long since finished washing up; there was now no sound in the apartment.

Nick had asked her a couple of times how she liked New York; how she liked her roommates. She had told him how clever it had been of him to pick just the right spot. He had asked her other questions, too, about her home with her grandfather, her trips to Europe, her friends in Buffalo. He knew quite a lot about her, Torre decided.

But she had not felt the same freedom to ask him questions. She knew he was older than herself—probably about twenty-seven, because he had been to college and had spent some time in service. She did not know what branch of the service, but she gained the impression he had been in the Air Force.

Going to the movies tonight with Marion Fenton had been, she admitted to herself, an underhanded attempt to learn more about Nick Tyler. Marion did something in the advertising department and was delighted to go to the movies. She confessed, over a sandwich in a drugstore, that she had wanted to know Torre better, but felt she was too "high hat."

"But that's ridiculous!" Torre protested.

"Somebody said your grandfather owns the company."

"Yes. He founded it." To Torre, it had never seemed important, but she could understand it might give someone the idea she *was* "high hat." But there was no use pursuing the subject further; she turned the conversation back to the office and her boss, Nick Tyler. Here again she found herself up against a caste system she had not dreamed existed.

"Mr. Tyler doesn't shout and get red in the face when he's mad, the way *my* boss does," was Marion's comment. "But he's probably just as unreasonable. Bosses are all alike."

So she learned nothing more about Nick, and probably it was for the best. She might have picked up some misinformation; a rumor without foundation in fact. Torre resolved that hereafter she would confine her questions about Nick to the boss himself.

She smiled as she thought of going in the next morning and saying brightly: "Would you like to tell me about your love life? Were you ever engaged? Are you going steady now?"

How silly can I get? Torre thought, and promptly fell asleep.

There was a note on the typewriter the next morning. Nick had gone on a business trip for a week or ten days. He would like to make his headquarters at a hotel in Chicago; in case of emergency, he told her—

A pity he and Rad Farnsworth can't get together, Torre thought crossly and then remembered Cindy had made a point of telling her that Rad was returning today and she had a date with him tonight.

The rest of the note contained a suggestion. Why didn't she arrange to go to the Public Library on Fifth Avenue and Forty-second Street and look through the books on architecture? He had already mentioned it to the president of the company, and she could spend the afternoons at the Library; the architecture room closed at five o'clock, he thought. Most of his correspondence would be handled by other departments, or could be held until his return.

The more Torre thought about it, the more alluring the idea seemed. She knew where the Library was; in fact, she had meant to visit it before. It was with a mounting sense of excitement that she raced through her work and then stepped off the bus to stand for a moment in front of the smirking lions.

You needn't feel so superior, she told the one looking down his nose at her. I'm going to be as smart as you are, some day.

It was like walking into another world, Torre felt as she crossed the marble floor to the information desk. Here was the very source of knowledge and inspiration. Anyone who approached with an open mind and eagerness to learn must go away the richer. And she had ten whole days!

Although it seemed like such a long time, Torre soon found the days went so quickly that the hours were not long enough. The mornings ceased to count; the work was routine and undemanding. But the afternoons, in the hushed room with the quiet, understanding librarian who seemed to realize there was an urgency about her studies the other students didn't have, were the highlights of her days.

Even her roommates faded into the background. Torre had asked to keep the "pad" in the dressing room for her own. And whether she ate out, or shared a meal with Veda and Cindy, she usually retired to her room and sketched until bedtime, working from the notes she had made that afternoon.

"Couldn't we mount some of your sketches and put them up in the living room?" asked Veda, openly admiring. "They seem terribly good to me."

"A good idea," Cindy agreed. "We could stand a decoration or two. It must be wonderful," she added wistfully, "to have everything: a wealthy grandfather, and talent, too!"

This remark Cindy had made, still rankled when Torre picked up the phone on Friday morning. The fact that Gander had money made no difference in her love for him; she could never measure her affection in terms of cash. And she was humbly aware of the smallness of her talent; she would have to work hard to make it count.

"Miss Torre Sherrill? Jacques Millet here—remember me?"

There was no mistaking the velvety voice, with its hint of amusement.

"Of course, Jac. I haven't forgotten what a good time we had on the Sky Ride."

"I've been trying to get you all week," Jac complained. "Your hours seem as unpredictable as mine, which is saying something."

"I've been out every afternoon." Torre was puzzled. "What did you want to call me about? Don't tell me the French Consulate is interested in Sealtight Siding!"

Jac laughed. "Only this member of it, and my interest is purely selfish. I'd like to take you out to dinner again. Have you been to the Hawaiian Pavilion at the Fair?"

"No," admitted Torre. "But I've heard about it." She was trying to decide what to do. Cindy had been very angry when she had dated Jac before, yet surely—since they were not engaged—there was no harm in going to dinner. She said quietly:

"You know we call Cindy our 'Fair Girl' at the apartment."

"I'm sure she knows all about it," Jac said smoothly. "But I haven't seen much of it, and I would like to see *you* again. How about tonight?"

Torre hesitated only a second longer. "Why not?" she asked. "I'll break down and tell you where I go every afternoon: the Public Library. Meet me there?"

"Right in front of a lion," Jac said cheerfully, and rang off.

Torre was still a little worried when Veda called to explain she was working late on a special report. Perhaps Torre would like to eat out, or bring something in for herself. Cindy had called and said she was going to a show with Rad Farnsworth, Veda went on, so Torre could make her plans to suit herself.

The fact that Cindy had a date made Torre feel better; when she met Jac Millet in front of the Library she felt a mounting sense of excitement. Whether it was because she was going to the Fair or because Jac was waiting for her, she did not pause to question.

"I know why you want to go the Hawaiian Pavilion," she accused him. "You want to see the hula."

"I've seen it," retorted Jac, "on its native heath— which is now our fiftieth state. But I've never seen eyes as big and blue as yours. That's what I'll be looking at instead of at the dancing—your eyes."

"You say that to all the girls," chided Torre, but she felt pleased and happy and ready for an evening of fun.

If Jac didn't gaze at the hula girls spell-bound, he was the only one in the Pavilion who didn't, Torre thought some time later. The dancing went on even after the delightfully exotic food was set before them, and she had to stop eating to watch.

"The dancing girls enjoy it themselves," she marveled.

"Not as much as the customers," Jac said, smiling. "That fat fellow over there is practically choking on his mouthful of poi."

"I can't be bothered watching the customers," Torre said gaily. "I'm having too much fun watching the dancers."

"I took only a side glance at his table," Jac said hastily. "You go ahead and have fun watching the dancers, and I'll have fun watching you!"

Chapter 8

The carved white jade earrings Jac Millet had bought for Torre at the Hong Kong Pavilion framed her face charmingly. Nick Tyler found it hard to concentrate on his dictation next morning. The earrings swung with every movement as Torre bent over her stenographer's pad, sometimes touching her cheek, sometimes outlined against her dark hair. Finally Nick gave up.

"Your earrings," he said as he concluded a letter, "are most becoming. Did you get them at the Fair?"

"Jac Millet bought them for me," answered Torre, a note of pride in her voice. "They're lovely, aren't they?"

Nick gazed thoughtfully at the animated face. "You had a good time in Hong Kong?" he asked.

It was all the encouragement Torre needed to launch into an excited account of the events of the evening before.

"We walked over the Bridge of the Rainbow above the Lagoon of the Emeralds," she began. "Then we found ourselves in a Chinese garden with rock settings. Veda will have to see that," she interrupted her description to say.

"Quite a place," said Nick politely.

"And in the middle of the garden there's a Chinese pagoda which has three floors, one of them a dance floor. We danced our feet off."

Nick's smile was strained. Torre did not notice that but chattered on.

"Everybody ate at little tables on the graveled terrace around the pagoda. The food was divine."

"Jac Millet seems to have been the perfect host," said Nick. Something in his tone made Torre say defensively:

"Well, he was! And we had a nice long talk—all about my plans for a career in architecture and my home in Buffalo and Gander and me being such pals. He said that was sort of unusual, a busy tycoon like Gander being a real friend to his granddaughter. And he said, 'I bet your grandfather will leave all his money to you!' "

"Very discerning of him,' observed Nick.

Torre laughed. "I told him Gander wasn't a tycoon. He isn't, you know. Then he said a funny thing. He said, 'Your grandfather is a millionaire, isn't he?' I said I didn't know. I never thought of him in that way, and in any case, he wasn't a tycoon. But Jac said, 'He sounds like a tycoon to me.' Wasn't that funny? Imagine calling darling Gander a tycoon!"

"I could die laughing," said Nick.

Torre looked at him sharply. "You don't like Jac, do you?"

"From what I've seen of him, and what you've told me about him, I'll give you a short answer—no. I think he's a fortune-hunter."

Torre laughed again. "But I haven't *got* a fortune!"

Nick ignored that. "Did your friend Jac ask you if you had any other relatives?"

"Yes, he did. And do you know, it turns out he's an orphan, like me. You'd feel sorry for him if you knew the way he was brought up—his parents died when he was young—by an old harridan of an aunt who didn't have children, wasn't even married, and who wouldn't have let him go to school at all except that the authorities made an uproar about it. . . ."

"I hope I don't have to begin feeling sorry for you," Nick interrupted.

Torre looked bewildered. "Why should you?"

"Skip it," said Nick grimly. "Some things a girl has to learn for herself, I guess." He stared at the white jade earrings. "I'm beginning to dislike those earrings," he remarked conversationally. "Yes, they definitely annoy me."

"In that case—" Torre spoke coldly, reaching up at the same time and taking them off—"I won't wear them —in the office." Her blue eyes darkened with resentment as she looked at Nick. "You're the boss."

"Please," said Nick, suddenly embarrassed, "I didn't mean to dictate what you wear. . . ."

Torre turned to a fresh page of her notebook and looked expectantly in Nick's direction, but at a point over his head.

"Never mind," said Nick. "I'm through with that kind of dictating, too, for the day." He smiled at his own jest, but it was a bleak smile. Torre didn't smile at all. She shut the book with a snap and rose. She had put the disturbing earrings in her lap, and as she rose, they slid to the floor. She bent to pick them up, at the very instant Nick also stooped to retrieve them. Their heads collided.

"Oh!" said Nick, standing up.

"Oh!" said Torre.

"I do beg your pardon," added Nick. "Did I hurt you?" He had the earrings in his hand and passed them over to Torre.

"Thanks," said Torre. "No, you didn't hurt me—only my feelings." She marched to the door, which was open, Nick tried to think of something to say that would detain her, but all he could think of was "goodbye," and he surely did not want to say *that*. As he stood tongue-tied, she vanished.

Veda had had a most unsettling experience at the Fair, she reported one evening at dinner time. It was one of the few evenings when the girls were eating at home, all together. Veda had been late in arriving, and Torre had about given her up when she appeared looking somewhat disheveled.

"I've practically been arrested for kidnapping!" she cried.

"You haven't been accused of kidnapping Wil Holland!" exclaimed Cindy. "He looks young, with all that blond hair and those guileless blue eyes, but not *that* young."

Veda frowned at her. Cindy had Wil on her mind, she was thinking.

"A little five-year-old boy," she announced, name of Darlington Wood—that's who I was accused of kidnapping."

"Darlington!" murmured the irresponsible Cindy. "Wait till he takes that name to school. The kindergarten set will probably murder him."

"Let Veda talk," admonished Torre. "Go on, Veda. Were you interrogated by the police, as they say in the news stories? And how come you were at the Fair today, instead of giving the Right-O! Cereal customers the benefit of your wiles?"

"Oh, I was working, in a way," explained Veda. "I had been sent to the Fair to check on the use of breakfast foods at different eating places. That's what I was doing when this little boy—tall for his age, though—started yelling. He was right at my heels, and he was screaming that his mother was lost."

"The little dear!" murmured Cindy, satirically.

"Well, he was a good-looking kid, as I found out afterward when I saw him with his mouth shut," said Veda. "But at the time all I could think of, his mouth was open so wide, and his face was so red, and he was yelling so loud, was that he'd have a fit if something wasn't done for him. So I did it. I took him to the RCA Color Center. It's just inside the main gate."

"Did he like the show?" inquired Torre. "It doesn't seem quite right to me, taking the kid off to a show when you should have called a guard or the police or somebody to find the kid's mother."

"That's all you know about the program entitled, 'Lost Kids at the Fair,'" observed Cindy. "The RCA people make a business of restoring lost kids to the arms of their frantic mothers, fathers, teachers or what have you. They put the child on screen, in color, and if his mother isn't merely deserting him, she'll hop over to the RCA Center and claim her cheeild."

"It sounds a pretty modern, not to say efficient way of finding lost children," said Torre. "We're just ready to eat. Are you hungry?"

"Starved," said Veda. "The spaghetti sauce smells great. I never suspected either of you girls of being handy with clam sauce for spaghetti."

"The sauce is Cindy's contribution," explained Torre. "She opened the can. I opened the can of spaghetti."

"Oh," said Veda, "I might have known. Wait till I wash my hands, and I'll be set to devour a large platter-ful."

"Hurry up," said Cindy. "What we want to know is what could possibly go wrong with the setup for lost children you were describing."

"Nothing went wrong with it," said Veda, returning and opening her paper napkin as she took her place at the table. "It worked like a charm. Mommie saw Darlington on TV and came running on the double. Tears were streaming down her cheeks as she attempted to enfold her offspring in her arms. She let go suddenly, however, and shook him instead. We were all shocked. Then one of the men attendants near me whispered, 'He kicked her.'

"The little brat!" Cindy exclaimed.

"And do you know why?" asked Veda, looking around the table and over her forkful of properly wound spaghetti. "You'll never guess. Darlington didn't want to be found. He wanted to stay at the TV counter and be televised over and over again, and the mother turned on me. She said I'd lured the child with a promise to put him on television."

"*Had* you?" inquired Torre.

"Well, of course; it was the only way to shut him up. It seems Darlington is a television addict and he thought, apparently, I was promising him a life career on a nationwide hookup."

"I don't think you should go wandering about the Fair alone, Veda," said Cindy severely. "Your good intentions so often backfire."

Veda sighed. "I really got in wrong with Darlington's mother. She made such an uproar somebody got hold of a special policeman. 'I want this baby-snatcher arrested,' Mama screeched, 'It's an outrage—she ought to be banned from the Fair. . . .' It took half a dozen attendants to spring me. That is, I wasn't jailed yet, but I expected to be at any minute. I was thinking I'd have to call Jacques Millet. If he's with the French Consulate, as I think you said, Cindy, he'd know how to get me out of the jam."

"Did you call him?" demanded Cindy suspiciously.

"No, of course not," said Veda. "It wasn't quite as bad as the way I'm telling it."

"It seems to me," said Cindy to no one in particular, "that Jacques Millet is the first man anybody thinks of when *anything* happens. In your case, Veda, it would have been the sensible thing for you to call up somebody at the Right-O! Cereal Company to get help; not to call another girl's fiancé."

"Fiancé!" cried Veda and Torre in chorus. Both looked hastily at Cindy's left hand. There was no ring in evidence.

"Jac is getting the ring very soon," explained Cindy. "The jeweler he went to—a friend of his—didn't have a diamond of the size he wanted in stock, and he's ordering it special."

Torre remembered when Jac had bought the earrings, he had said he adored jade, and if and when he got engaged to marry, he'd buy the girl a magnificent jade engagement ring. He had said he did not like diamonds.

"Coffee, anyone?" asked Cindy, getting up to bring the percolator from the stove in the tiny kitchenette. Both Veda and Torre pushed their cups toward her but made no comment about an out-sized diamond for an apparently mythical engagement ring.

The phone rang. Cindy put the percolator on the table and answered so quickly that neither of the other girls had time to get up. Cindy always answered if possible. Even if the caller wanted one of the other girls, she managed to exchange a few bits of badinage, if the caller were a man. But this call was for her.

"Rad!" she cried. "I didn't expect to hear from you tonight."

Then, apparently in answer to a question, "Of course I'm glad you did. Come over now? Well, the other girls—that's so; it's still early."

When she hung up she turned a bright face to the other two.

"Rad!" she exclaimed. "He'd date me every night if I'd let him."

"Maybe *he's* got an engagement ring for you," murmured Torre.

"The cattiness around here!" said Cindy coldly. "I've

got to get dressed. Red is meeting me at Grand Central; we'll taxi from there to the Fair."

"Too bad you've had your dinner. You could have eaten in some exotic place at the Fair," sighed Torre.

"We're going to the International Business Machines Exhibit," said Cindy. "There won't be time to eat, anyway. Something that happened during his business trip to Chicago made Rad anxious to see some of the new computer systems they're showing at the Fair."

A moment later a cry came from the bedroom, where Cindy was dressing.

"Torre, could you lend me a pair of stockings? I've got a run in my last pair."

Veda smiled at Torre. "Three engagement rings, according to her story, but no stockings."

Torre shrugged. "Oh, well, you know Cindy."

"To build the IBM Pavilion, it was necessary for these people to use their own computers," explained Conrad Farnsworth, when he and Cindy were on their way to the Fair by taxi. "The pavilion is eggshaped, and involved all sorts of unprecedented problems of stress and balance."

"What a challenge!" murmured Cindy, mentally doing a little computation of her own. How much money, for instance, did Wil Holland really have? She remembered finally to thank Rad for the dinosaur.

"It was good of you to think of me, darling," said

Cindy. She was usually sparing of endearments with Rad—no use letting him get the wrong impression about her feelings, in case a better marriage prospect should materialize. To her surprise, Rad appeared not to notice at all her affectionate "darling."

"Why wouldn't I think of you?" he said matter-of-factly. "We've known each other for—let's see now, how long is it?"

Cindy knew exactly how long Conrad had been dating her, without any definite suggestion of marriage up to now. If a wealthy man eluded her within the next six months, it might be necessary to encourage Rad—but really. The time had not yet come, however, so she answered Rad's question with a deprecating little laugh.

"Darling, I've no head for figures. Maybe we can ask one of those computers we're going to see tonight."

Chapter 9

The evening with Rad Farnsworth passed off much as other evenings had as far as Cindy was concerned. There always came a moment when the very sound of Rad's voice going on and on about some dull topic— usually one connected with bookkeeping or some type of statistics—bored her to the point of tears. She would usually let her mind wander away from what he was saying, and when Rad noticed she would smile and confess that she was a little tired.

Then, on the way home in a taxi, Rad would try to kiss her. She had various defenses against being kissed. Sometimes she would simply return to her statement that she was too tired to feel romantic; sometimes she would start him talking again about his favorite topic; sometimes she would simply say, "No, please!" sometimes she would let him kiss her—a cool antiseptic type of salute.

But Cindy was thinking, as she stood behind the polished counter of the hotel, an evening with Rad

Farnsworth was anything but exciting. Now Jac Millet, on the other hand, made an evening interesting and thrilling. Of course Jac did not not answer her definition of a rich man, but in the diplomatic service there was no telling how far a man could go. If he had position, perhaps money wouldn't matter so very much.

Of course Cindy's thoughts never showed on her face. She was a trained model, and in her special uniform she always looked cool and serene and quite above the common, ordinary, run-of-the-mill problems of daily living. She was aware as she looked up at the bald, middle-aged man who was standing in front of the counter that he would have been shocked to discover how far afield her thoughts were. Cindy noted automatically that his suit was good but had been ready-made; that the diamond ring he wore was a good stone and fairly large, but was undoubtedly merely a status symbol in the small town were he probably lived. In other words, she had absolutely no interest in the man, but she knew exactly how to look at him under her lashes and ask sweetly:

"What can I do for you, sir?"

"I can think of a lot of things you could do for me," the man said heartily, with an evident attempt to be quite devilish. "You could come out to the Fair with me. I'm all alone here in the big city. I'm from Syracuse: 'a Boy from Syracuse.' That is the title of a play, you know. Get it?"

"I hope you enjoy your visit with us." Cindy's words were cold, but she softened them with a warm smile. "What was it you wished to ask, sir?"

Encouraged, when he had expected a rebuff, the man carefully laid his pudgy hand on the counter. Without seeming to notice, Cindy moved a pile of folders so that her hands were quite a distance away.

"I thought I'd like to see what this Monorail thing is," the man said. Cindy was fairly sure he was just making conversation, but she saw the assistant hotel manager in the distance, and so she responded cordially:

"I'm so glad you asked that question. I believe it is one of the most thrilling sights at the World's Fair. Actually, the Monorail is suspended forty feet above the ground on two parallel tracks. It's an exciting way to see the Amusement Area of the Fair. For instance, way up in the air you can look down on Dancing Waters, on the puppet theater, on the boats on Meadow Lake—and one of them is the replica of the *Santa Maria*."

"You mean one of the ships that came over here when Columbus discovered America?" The "Boy from Syracuse" appeared delighted to show off his historical knowledge.

"The *Santa Maria* was Columbus' idea of a space ship," Cindy said, with a throaty little laugh that made it a joke for him alone. Actually, she had used the line many times. "Of course the Monorail is newer than a sailing ship; it runs on electric motors which supply the power."

Judging the man had been unduly encouraged, Cindy's expression became aloof and reserved. Anyway, the assistant manager had disappeared from the lobby.

"I don't really care about this Monorail. If you'd like to go somewhere else, say, some of those fancy restaurants where they have a floor show—you just name it—I'm in the mood to paint the town red tonight."

The assistant manager suddenly appeared on the other side of the lobby. He came and went, Cindy thought resentfully, like an ill wind. She forced herself to smile at the pudgy man across from her even as she said:

"I'm not allowed to accompany the hotel guests to the Fair," she explained in a low tone. "It's one of the very strict rules of the hotel. But thank you, anyway, for the invitation."

"Say, you don't have to worry about me," the pudgy man said, lowering his voice to a confidential rumble. "I wouldn't want you to get into any trouble about your job. But I've been watching you, and you must be getting through pretty soon. You've been here since this morning."

Cindy hastily revised her type of brush-off. Usually when one of the guests was importunate and she did not want to go out with him, she picked a distant hour and said she would not be free to leave until that time.

But this impossible guy had evidently watched her when she came on duty. And the assistant manager was talking to the clerk at the airlines reservation desk. She played for time.

"No, really, I'm afraid I can't go out with you tonight."

"Aw, don't be like that," the man admonished. "I'll wait outside the lobby—near that third entrance over there. Or I can meet you anywhere you say."

"No, really, I'm afraid it will be quite impossible." Cindy watched as the assistant manager left the reservation desk and disappeared down the corridor. She turned back toward the pudgy man, and her expression froze the tentative smile on his face.

"You see," Cindy said firmly, "I have relatives in Syracuse. My sister lives there, and I visit her quite often. Her husband owns the newspaper, you know," Cindy said, with an air of confiding frankness, "and it's remarkable the way he keeps track of their readers who go off to New York. Why, I remember once—"

But she was speaking to thin air. The pudgy man had turned a slow brick-red, had swallowed once, hard, and then had turned and walked with hurried steps through the lobby and out into the street. Cindy smiled to herself. The Number Three brush-off never failed to work. Sometimes her "sister" lived in St. Louis or Minneapolis, depending on the town from which the visitor came. Sometimes her nonexistent sister had only to be mentioned and the lonely visitor would vanish. But if she wanted to be really firm, she always made the same remark about her sister being married to the owner of the newspaper. It was a sure way to discourage any would-be Lothario.

It was several days later before Jac Millet finally called Cindy and asked for a date. Cindy was never one to thrive on neglect, and she had been by turns annoyed, displeased and angry with Jac for making her wait so long between dates. She was quite sure he was seeing another girl, and the thought made her furious. She even phoned him at the French Consulate, but she did not leave her name when she found Jac was not in.

She was particularly annoyed because she had spent more money than she should have on a new outfit of cream-colored, lightweight wool. It was perfectly plain, with a tuck suggesting a low waistline and a cuffed collar that flowed gently around the base of her throat. She had been unable to resist an exaggerated Breton of white felt that made her face look like a carved cameo. She had bought the outfit especially for Jac's benefit, and for quite a while it had seemed she had wasted her money.

But all at once he called. He would meet her in the lobby of the hotel at five-thirty. Cindy did a quick calculation. She would be off duty at four o'clock, so she would have time to return to the apartment, shower and then meet Jac in the lobby at the specified time, glamorous in her new costume. She had made a date with Rad Farnsworth, and she tried to reach him, but learned he would not be back in the office until after six, if at all. Cindy shrugged. She would explain it some other time to Rad.

Her timetable worked out beautifully. At exactly five-twenty-five she slipped into the lobby from a side door and walked across the plush carpets as if she were one of the guests. The hotel lobby was almost deserted at that hour; the girl behind her counter, recognizing her, smiled and nodded her approval of the new oufit. Cindy walked over to the revolving door, wondering if Jac meant to wait for her outside. She stepped into one of the sections and pushed against the panel. But she could not move it. As she looked up at the man who was in the next section and pushing against the door in the opposite direction, she gazed into the laughing dark eyes of Jac Millet. She stood for a second smiling at him, and then, all at once, a large hand descended on Jac's shoulder, and he was spun around and rushed out of the door.

Simultaneously, with the opposing pressure gone, the revolving door whirled under Cindy's hand and ejected her onto the street in a stumbling run. She all but collided with Rad Farnsworth, whose big hand clutched the slim shoulder of Jac Millet.

"Rad!" she cried. "What in the name of goodness

do you think you're doing?"

"This joker," said Rad grimly, "is playing tricks with a revolving door. I ought to punch him in the nose."

Cindy stamped her foot angrily. "Let him go, you big oaf," she said furiously. "He's a friend of mine."

Rad released Jac, who shrugged his shoulders and pulled his jacket straight where Rad's clutch had twisted it.

"And who is your friend?" Rad demanded, although he looked unsure of himself in the face of Cindy's anger. Cindy introduced them and added: "Jac has asked me to have dinner with him at the Fair."

"I thought we had a date," Rad Farnsworth said, looking not so much aggrieved as bewildered.

"You got mixed up," Cindy said blandly. "Our date was for tomorrow night."

"Oh!" Rad said, backing away. "I'm sorry," he mumbled to Jac.

"Think nothing of it," said Jac, taking Cindy's arm and smiling down at her fondly. "Sorry, old boy. I guess this isn't your night. Better luck next time."

As he guided Cindy along the sidewalk toward the taxi stand at the corner, she was thinking to herself that it had been quite an eye-opening occasion for Jac Millet. Rad Farnsworth was obviously a devoted admirer and abjectly crestfallen at having to give up his date. Yes, it wouldn't hurt Jac a bit to know that all the while he hadn't phoned, she had not been sitting home waiting for him; she could have had as many dates as she wanted with someone else. She felt a great tenderness toward Rad welling up in her. She turned and looked back over her shoulder to where Rad Farnsworth still stood in front of the revolving door, the picture of dejection.

"Bye now," she called softly.

Cindy let herself into the apartment at almost two o'clock in the morning. Veda and Torre were both asleep. But Veda had pulled out the day bed, so all Cindy had to do was get undressed and climb in between the cool sheets.

The evening had not been a success from her point of view. Oh, she had enjoyed herself, and she was sure Jac had had a good time. But still the net result was a baffled feeling. They had had dinner at the Port of New York Authority restaurant, called the Top of the Fair, and both the view and the food had been superb. But Cindy had other things than an evening of diversion on her mind. She began by asking directly:

"What do you do at the French Consulate, Jac? You've never really told me, you know. I don't know if you speak French."

"I speak French," Jac assured her. "My mother and father and my aunt came from Normandy. It's a wonderful way to make love—the French language. There are so many special endearments that would sound silly or stilted in English but that give a feeling of romance when they are said in French."

Jac, his eyes dancing, reached over and covered her hand with his. Then he said in his velvety voice so many French phrases that Cindy could only look at him in wonder. Even to her untutored ear Jac was well qualified for his job at the French Consulate, on the basis of language alone.

"I had only one year of French in high school," Cindy admitted, blushing, when he finally stopped. "But I suspect one of your endearments was calling me a little cabbage, and I don't think that is particularly romantic."

She remembered afterward that Jac had very cleverly avoided telling her what his work was. Later when they were dancing she had tried again.

"The reason I asked about your job," she said with her cheek pressed against his shoulder, "is that I had a dreadful feeling when I didn't hear from you. Maybe you had been sent to France, I was thinking."

"And would you miss me?" Jac asked.

"Of course." Cindy felt a sinking sensation as she realized what she had said was true. She had been determined to marry a moneyed man, but somehow, with Jac, money did not seem so important. At any rate, she knew now she would be willing to trade it for the position and prestige of having a husband in a diplomatic post. But it was no part of Cindy's plan to let Jac know how serious she was.

"I would miss you as a playmate," she said lightly.

"I could be sent to France," Jac admitted. "In fact, I am eager to go. But don't let's talk about my leaving. Tonight we are together—the moon rides high, and maybe I am a little bit in love with you."

This was the type of conversational sparring Cindy was used to. "Only a little bit?"

"Only a little bit tonight, maybe a little bit more tomorrow, maybe much, much more next week. Who knows?" Jac shrugged. "That is the reason it is so difficult to make love in English. The British and of course the Americans, too, like to analyze love and take it apart and see what makes it work. You don't treat love as an emotion. You treat it as a streetcar that you are forever running after and trying to catch."

Cindy was annoyed. It was Jac's diplomatic training, she supposed, which made it so difficult to pin him down to a straight answer to a straight question.

"You are an American," she said sharply.

"Ah, but when it comes to love I am not half French. I am all French. There is a little difference."

"Vive la différence!"

Cindy had given up any attempt at serious conversation after that, and Jac had set himself to be most amusing and attentive, so that for the next few hours Cindy had forgotten everything but the pleasure of being entertained.

It was only now, lying in the quiet apartment, with

her eyes shut and courting sleep, that she realized how hopeless was her prospect of marrying Jac. It was ironic, she thought, that when she found one man with whom she could have been happy even without money, that one man made it quite clear that his intentions, at least as far as she was concerned, had nothing to do with marriage.

Chapter 10

Torre was at her typewriter, busily transcribing notes, when Nick Tyler, at his desk between two immense windows of the office, spoke briefly into the intercom and then glanced over at Torre.

"There's a gentleman to see me in the reception room," he called. "Will you see what he wants, Torre?"

As a rule, callers were screened in the outer office by the receptionist herself, and Torre was surprised to be sent on this kind of errand. She rose immediately. A tall, distinguished-looking white-haired man came forward as she entered the reception room. Torre took one look and ran to throw herself into his arms.

"Gander!"

Nick Tyler had followed Torre, and now he smiled a welcome to the founder of the firm and introduced himself. They all went back to Nick's office.

The talk that followed was a mixture of recent company figures and comparisons with former years' figures and interpolations of: "How is my little girl getting along?" and "Hard work seems to agree with her; she looks twice as blooming as when she left Buffalo."

In time Torre discovered that her grandfather was in New York to perfect plans for an outing at the Fair for the benefit of his favorite charity. Members of the organization were paying a subscription of twenty-five dollars for the charity, with the privilege of joining the Fair outing.

"Everything's ready," said Simon Sherrill; "the response has been fine. I've arranged a package deal, pro-rated among them, covering transportation, hotel rooms for two nights, meals and so on. In addition, each one has bought a ticket for the Fair, which they paid for and which I had specially printed. Each ticket covers transportation to and from Manhattan to the Fair, dinner at the Polynesian Pavilion, several rides and visits to certain exhibits, all of which were decided on by vote back home."

"And you're to be the guide?" asked Nick.

"Oh no, one of the ladies is taking charge, the president of the charity, the *League for Country Vacations for Underprivileged Children*. She has everything figured out, with the subscription price, and the whole affair amounts to less than a hundred dollars each. We expect a lot of fun for the money, as well as substantial benefit to the charity."

"Much more fun to be going to the Fair with a lot

of people you know," put in Torre.

"You'd like to be in on it yourself, wouldn't you, Sugar?" Simon Sherrill asked her.

"I'd love it!" cried Torre.

Her grandfather grinned at her affectionately. "That's what I was hoping. While you've been slaving away down here, I've been trying to think of some special kind of good time for you. So I've taken subscriptions for you and your roommates—and their boy friends, if they have any—and Nick, and bought six extra for amusements at the Fair."

He brought out an envelope and handed it to Torre. "There's the whole package of fun and enlightenment for you and your pals."

Torre threw her arms around her grandfather's neck.

"Gander, you honey of a grandfather!" she cried. "If only I could do something nice for you!"

"Seeing you happy is enough for me," said Simon Sherrill, pressing his lined cheek against her smooth one.

"Now I've got to run," he said after a moment. "I've got a board meeting this afternoon. I may be retired," he added to Nick, "but I still have a finger in a good many financial pies. After that there's a testimonial dinner, and tomorrow I have a busy day with my lawyers."

He made Torre write down the name of the hotel where he was staying, just in case she needed him in a hurry, and gave her directions for joining the party at the chartered buses that would be waiting for them at six o'clock in the evening near Times Square.

"Isn't he a love?" Torre asked Nick, when her grandfather had gone. "Two lovely tickets to the Fair."

"Are you going to keep them both?" Nick inquired. "After all, I practically arranged this party, and I'm sure your grandfather expects me to go with you."

"Perhaps my grandfather takes too much for granted," Torre murmured. "There *is* such a thing as paying your own way."

"Do you have a boy friend?" Nick demanded. He sounded genuinely alarmed.

"And what if I do?" Torre retorted. "Am I so unattractive?"

"You're too darned attractive, and you know it," Nick said sharply. "And whether you ask me to be your date at Mr. Sherrill's party or not, I'm going to be right behind you and this secret pal of yours—every step of the way!"

Cindy and Veda were delighted with the invitation to Simon Sherrill's "gala," as Cindy called it.

"You two ask anyone you want," Torre said, and waited to see if either one would announce she would bring Jacques Millet. But both Cindy and Veda were silent. And all night, and all the next day, Torre had visions of having her gala spoiled by watching someone, probably Cindy, with Jac at the Fair. As a matter of fact, the suave young man did have two invitations to join the party. Cindy called him first.

Jacques Millet listened with interest to Cindy's account of Simon Sherrill's proposed evening at the Fair. He had almost said yes when he learned he would be expected to join a large party of solid citizens from out of town and listen to their banal comments. The thought of seeing Torre's grandfather, who was probably a shrewd old duck and would suspect him of fortune-hunting, also made him shudder. He promptly explained to Cindy how heartbroken he was, but a consulate meeting—

Cindy did not believe his excuse, but she accepted it and immediately called Rad Farnsworth. He said he would be delighted to come.

Torre, feeling guilty at calling Jac instead of inviting Nick Tyler, was trembling with excitement as she dialed the number where Jac could be reached mornings. It wasn't exactly the Consulate, he had told her, but a private wire they preferred him to use. "So much official business, you know. . . ."

Jac was in. He sounded irritated when he answered the phone. He was still smarting at having had to decline Cindy's invitation, and wondered if he could accept Torre's, if one should be forthcoming. There might be some way of luring Torre away from the rest of that tiresome party. But no, on second thought,

Torre's grandfather probably would not let her out of his sight.

Torre, of course, having no idea that Cindy had already given him a blueprint of what the evening would be like, put Jac's irritation down to the press of international affairs. She was apologizing meekly for interrupting him when, forestalling what he foresaw was an invitation to "Old Man Sherrill's wingding," Jac told her he was leaving at once for Washington and was already late.

"But I always love to hear your voice, sweet," he said, "and it would be wonderful to see you this evening if only this Washington conference—"

She understood, Torre said, and hung up without mentioning the gala. What was the use? He couldn't come.

Veda had a different experience. She simply called Wil Holland, who sounded enthusiastic about the party. Well, that was the way Wil was—always cooperative. But nevertheless Veda breathed a sigh of relief; Cindy might have gotten to Wil first and made the date without letting him know that she, Veda, was to be in the party.

Torre and Nick taxied to the meeting place on a side street near Times Square the next afternoon. Simon Sherrill was standing on the sidewalk talking with one of the bus drivers—two buses had been chartered—and he hugged Torre affectionately when they arrived, and shook hands with Nick. Both vehicles were almost full, but space had been reserved for the three girls and their escorts.

Simon Sherrill himself sat in a front seat with the chairwoman, who was introduced to Torre and Nick as Mrs. Alonzo Fairlee.

"I know Torre," Mrs. Fairlee interrupted. "My Debbie has a boy baby now," she reported.

"How nice for her," I must send the baby a present."

Veda and Cindy, Wil and Rad, were already seated, with an empty seat left behind them for Torre and Nick. Cindy must have had her hair done that day, Torre reflected, wondering how she had managed to get the time off from her job. It shone like pale, polished gold. And she was wearing a dress Torre had never seen before—probably bought today, too, Torre thought. It was a startling Kelly green knit silk shift with a turtle neck and no sleeves; it showed off her lovely tall figure to perfection. She looked every inch the model she had been. Torre noticed other passengers in the bus also kept glancing Cindy's way.

By contrast, she and Veda were far from eye-catching, as far as their clothes were concerned. Torre had a white cotton suit—short jacket and tight skirt—trimmed with navy and magenta braid. She had worn it several times to work, and it had been to the laundry more than once. Veda's beige and black linen jacket over a beige linen sheath was becoming, but unspectacular. Torre noticed, however, that Wil Holland seldom turned his head away from her. From where she sat, it looked to Torre as if Wil's eyes were fastened on Veda's face. He reminded her of a great, clumsy blond sheep dog she had once seen in a picture.

The Polynesian Village restaurant had been decided upon as the place where the group was to have dinner that night. Other exhibits they had agreed to take in, en masse, were the New York State County Fair of the Future; the Pavilion of Spain—to see the Spanish dancers; the Travelers Insurance exhibit—showing man's progress through the centuries; various rides; a visit to the Indian Village and to the World's Fair Marina, where the *Santa Maria*, a replica of Columbus' ship, was anchored.

The buses were rolling. Torre, with most of the other out-of-towners who were from Buffalo like herself, watched the passing scene with avid attention. Their route took them to the Fifty-ninth Street bridge and over it to Queens Boulevard; the driver called out the street names as they made the turns. They finally reached the Long Island Expressway, which led directly to the Fair grounds. The trip was scheduled, the driver said, to take forty-five minutes.

"He's doing it in less, I think," said Nick, as they neared their destination. "Here we are, and it took us only forty minutes!"

Glida-Ride trains carried Simon Sherrill's party to "Polynesia," where the "long house" restaurant in the center of the village overlooked a tropical lagoon. Torre and Nick were milling about with the others, looking for a place to sit, when Torre felt a touch on her arm.

"It's Torre Sherrill, isn't it?" The large, angular woman who had touched her arm was smiling; as least the contorted features of the angular face were simulating a smile, as Torre recognized the woman as an acquaintance from back home.

"I'm so glad I met you," Mrs. Purcell gushed, patting Torre's cheek—a gesture she detested. "Benjy heard you were working in New York and he's been hoping to run into you every time he comes down. He's a buyer in men's wear now—the same store he worked in when he used to date you."

"I'm glad to hear it," murmured Torre, wishing she could escape. Nick was eyeing her with such a grave expression she knew he must be amused by the encounter. "Look!" she cried suddenly. "There are the Samoan dancers! Aren't they graceful?"

But Mrs. Purcell was not to be distracted. "Will you give me your telephone number, dear? Benjy will want to call you."

Reluctantly, Torre gave her the number. She would have preferred leaving her renewed acquaintance with Benjy to a chance encounter—happily remote—on the city streets. But Mrs. Purcell was a leader in civic organizations, and she dared not alienate her. When Veda beckoned to a place beside her, Torre muttered a hasty, "Excuse me; see you later," and, seizing Nick's arm, made a run for it toward her roommate.

"Benjy," remarked Nick, grinning at Torre when they were seated, "is one of the reasons you left Buffalo, I gather."

"Please," implored Torre, "don't mention the name to me. I made the mistake of dating Benjy once, and ever since he persisted in trying to date me again. I almost beat my brains out thinking up new ways to refuse him. If he tracks me down here, I'll tell him I'm engaged to be married, my fiancé is the jealous type, and he won't let me even say hello to old friends."

It was a good opening, Nick saw, for a discussion of Torre's ideas about romantic understandings. Did she favor long or short engagements, for instance? But, he told himself sternly, such discussions were out for the time being. Torre was Simon Sherrill's granddaughter; he was only an employee.

Nick was so busy facing the miserable reality of being deeply in love with Torre and at the same time determined not to show it, he had to be nudged by Veda before he noticed what was going on in front of his unseeing eyes.

"Those Polynesian girls are diving for pearls in the lagoon," she whispered, "and you're not even looking!"

"Oh, sure—I see them," retorted Nick. "But I thought

they were only diving for oysters."

Torre, on his other side, giggled. "They're pearl-bearing oysters, silly," she said, "and you can buy them."

"You can?" asked Nick cheering up. "Maybe I can buy three: one pearl on a half shell for each of you girls."

If he bought pearls for Veda and Cindy, too, it wouldn't be exactly an intimate gift for Torre, he told himself. On the other hand, Torre couldn't refuse to take hers if the other girls accepted the pearls. He had never dared offer her a gift before, and the prospect of giving her one exhilarated him. Now, if Cindy's Rad and Veda's Wil suggested having their pearls set in rings, Torre would most certainly have to permit him to do likewise!

He thought of Torre taking dictation with his pearl ring on her finger—the third finger. Not the engagement finger, of course. But still he felt a warm glow as he pictured the pearl, lustrous against her pale hand. Pearls, he decided, would suit Torre. If only he could afford to give her a pearl necklace!

"Don't you love this exotic food?" said Torre, interrupting his bright dream.

"Wha—oh, yes, the food. Great!" Nick could have been eating sawdust for all the attention he had paid to chicken served in a cocoanut shell, baked bananas, some type of fish and other unfamiliar and quite luscious dishes. He eyed the Tahitian girl dancers with totally

uninterested eyes; they were merely part of the entertainment, to be sat through until it was time to buy the
oysters-with-pearls.

It was disappointing, when the time came, to find
they were small pearls, not resembling in the least the
king-sized beauties he had been mentally picturing.
The girls accepted them joyfully, however.

"How sweet of Nick!" said Cindy.

"He's a living doll!" said Veda.

"It's a darling pearl," said Torre.

Nothing was said about having the tiny pearls set
in rings.

Chapter 11

The IBM Pavilion was fun, Wil suddenly announced.
Over there they could see a film, a puppet show, a
musical tower with a message and a computer translat-
ing Russian into English instantly."

"I didn't know you were interested in computers,"
Veda said, with a longing glance back at the Polynesian
Pavilion, which they were leaving.

"Figures," said Wil Holland firmly, "mathematics,
that is, has always been a romantic subject." He piloted
her skillfully through the crowd.

He was like a small boy let loose in a toy shop. His
eyes brightened with enjoyment from the minute the
elevating grandstand lifted them and the other four
hundred and ninety-eight visitors fifty-three feet above
the pavilion roof and into the ovoid theater. Wil hurled
statistics at her, and all Veda could do was to nod
numbly. It was almost like being back in the office, she
reflected.

"This twelve-minute film we are going to see on nine

screens makes complex computing as simple as a bank statement," Wil added solemnly.

"One of those machines can tell how many people will get married in New York City during the next year."

"Given the right material, I suppose they can figure out anything," Veda said, still slightly confused by Wil's interest in the subject.

"That computer there," Wil went on relentlessly, "demonstrates the theory of probability. Every eighteen minutes, seventeen thousand polyethylene balls drop twelve feet."

"They do?" murmured Veda.

"Marvelous, isn't it?" said Wil.

"Marvelous," Veda agreed. She had just caught sight of the typewriter bar, which afforded the free use of ten electric typewriters plus free postcards on which to write a message.

"Wouldn't you like to send a card to the one and only girl?" Veda said teasingly. To her surprise, Wil turned a dull brick-red. For some reason she seemed to have hit upon an embarrassing subject.

"I was only fooling," Veda said hastily, taking his arm. "Let's walk around and see some of the fountains."

"Are you sure you wouldn't like to look over the exhibit where Sherlock Holmes solves 'The Case of the Elusive Train' by using computer logic?"

Veda decided she had had enough. "I don't know

what's gotten into you, Wil Holland," she said firmly. "But you know darn well I get enough of facts and figures all day long. Yet you drag me away from Simon Sherrill's party to show me the marvels of electronic computers. Unless you can give me a sane reason for the way you are acting, I think perhaps we had better go back to the party."

"I can't give you a sane reason for anything tonight," Wil muttered, "but you're right. A mathematical background is not the proper setting for what I had in mind. Let's go and find one of the fountains you mentioned a few minute ago."

Wil Holland was a big man, and at the moment a determined one. He put his hand under her elbow, and she had no choice but to accompany him outside the pavilion and into the stream of pedestrians. Wil asked her politely if she had any special fountain in mind, and just as politely Veda told him that she had spoken at random. Any fountain would do.

They finally came upon a very beautiful fountain, illuminated with changing lights, with the soft music of a Viennese waltz as a background. Veda sank down on a bench, and Wil took his place beside her.

"You look very lovely tonight, Veda," he said, gazing at the fountain. "You're the prettiest girl here."

"Why, Wil!" Veda was genuinely surprised. Her acquaintance with Wil Holland had begun only a matter of weeks before. As a matter of fact, she had felt slightly self-conscious on her dates with him since he had told her about the various companies he had founded and was operating.

"That's why I took you to the IBM Pavilion," Wil said, and Veda felt she must have missed some part of the conversation.

"You took me to the IBM Pavilion because of the way I look tonight?" she questioned. "Probably I'm dense, but I don't see any connection."

"It's as simple as two and two make four," Wil said. He turned toward her, and Veda was amazed to see that he looked diffident and shy. "You are the prettiest girl here tonight, so naturally I am in love with you and want to marry you."

The suddenness of it took Veda's breath away. She had had one indefinite proposal back in Kansas City, but she was not prepared for this one. Somehow she had thought of a period of courtship—flowers, tender messages, even stolen kisses—before there was any talk of marriage.

Wil took out his handkerchief and mopped his brow, although the evening was cool. He seemed to be terribly in earnest, and all at once Veda smiled.

"I know it is a hackneyed phrase," Veda said at last, "but it's the only one I can think of: 'this is so sudden, Sir.'"

"It isn't sudden at all," Wil growled. "From the very first minute Jack Simmons brought me into your office,

I knew you were the only girl for me. I could have told you so right away, but I thought I would lead up to it gradually."

"Gradually!"

"Yes—you know, take you out to dinner, talk about things we both like, meet your roommates—the works."

"That doesn't seem to me a very gradual approach to a proposal of marriage," Veda objected. "Also, you're supposed to be engaged for a while and sort of talk things over. Marriage is a very serious step," she told him.

Wil grinned at her triumphantly. "At least I did one thing right," he said. "I bought the ring yesterday. We can be engaged right away." He took a small box out of his pocket and pressed the clasp. Even in the soft light the stone shimmered and sparkled.

"It looks like the water splashing in the fountain," Veda said, as he took her hand and slipped the ring on her finger.

"Since we are engaged—" Wil swept her into his arms and kissed her with determination.

When Veda at last managed to catch her breath and draw back a little, she protested:

"Wil! Right out here with everybody looking at us! You shouldn't."

"Why not?" Wil asked, pulling her close once more. "Everybody else is just jealous, darling!"

Torre and Cindy returned to the apartment together

slightly after midnight. Cindy was in a bad humor, and it was something of an effort for her to thank Torre for the evening of entertainment Simon Sherrill had provided.

"Did you see Veda after she walked off with Wil Holland?" asked Cindy. "Rad and I waited around, thinking she'd be back and we two could join them in seeing the prehistoric animals in the Ford Pavilion."

"Never saw her again," said Torre, "and she's not home yet. She and Wil must be doing the whole Fair. You must have enjoyed the cave-man bit and the City of Tomorrow and all that at the Ford spot, though, didn't you?"

"Well, of course. Only I wanted to see that water and air show in the Lake Amusement area, or Dick Button's Ice Extravaganza or even the circus—something that was just entertaining. I've been telling so many of the hotel visitors about these things that I've become wild to see them."

"The Fair will last awhile," said Torre. "But you must have got a charge out of seeing the cave men invent the wheel and create fire. I heard Rad telling you about it while we were eating Polynesian food."

"Oh, sure," said Cindy. "It was exciting enough. Rad has had a yen to see the life-sized dinosaurs ever since he sent me that replica from Chicago. We rode through time on Disney's Magic Skyway, you know, and we could see and hear the monsters moving around and fighting." She broke off to laugh as she slipped off her shoes and unzipped her frock.

"There were moments when I wished the dinos would escape and chase Rad around the Skyway or some place, just to liven things up. Would you believe it, we were riding in a convertible, and that Rad didn't even put his arm around me. I screamed when the cave man grunted, too, and what did Rad do? He just grinned at me. I can just imagine how it would have been if I'd been with Jac.

"Then I shuddered a little and said, 'Ooh! Suppose a guy like that wanted to date me. I'd have a conniption fit.' And Rad said, 'They're electric people with plastic skins. What it must take to keep them running.'"

Cindy began to set her hair, and Torre went off to take a shower. Cindy, sitting in front of the dressing table which was shared by all three girls, stared at her own charming face and mentally compared it with the cave man she had been watching that evening. Rad had enjoyed the show so much that he had insisted on seeing it three times.

"Those old frog faces!" Cindy had exclaimed, when Rad had announced his intention to check and double-check the show.

"I'm really fascinated," said Rad. "Imagine living without any way of making fire!"

"Where there's smoke there's fire," said Cindy flippantly.

"My dear girl! Don't you understand? There wasn't any smoke in those days."

Cindy was in a perverse mood. "Didn't lightning ever strike a tree or something?" she inquired, looking innocent. "If the cave man had the sense he was born with, he would have cut down the burning tree and made himself a nice bonfire."

"Don't be silly," was all Rad said.

Cindy wondered where Veda and Wil Holland had gone. And Torre and Simon Sherrill and Nick Tyler. And all the rest of the people in the Buffalo party. She wished she had stayed with them.

"Let's go to the amusement area," she said to Rad, "for a change of pace. We can come back here if you like."

"I'm interested in this exhibit. Just think, the strange spacecraft we are seeing here may be just familiar sights to us in a few years—or at least to our children."

"I don't believe my children will appreciate the wonders of air travel of the future," said Cindy. "It would be just like them to prefer underwater living."

But Rad wasn't listening. His eyes were glued to the battle of the prehistoric monsters.

"Slick, isn't it? Just wires and valves and bits of plastic. And we're back in the days before the dawn of history!"

Remembering Rad's enthusiastic voice and the sparkle in his eyes, Cindy, as she finished setting her hair, glanced over to the table where the dinosaur replica Rad had sent had been given a place of honor. She got up, advanced on the little model, and with one violent motion sent it flying across the room.

Torre came by just in time to see the gesture.

"Poor little Dino!" she exclaimed, running to pick up the replica. "You might have broken it."

"Impossible," said Cindy furiously. "It's plastic."

So Veda walked in on a tense tableau which she did not understand and which Cindy, after a first startled glance at her, decided she did not even notice. Veda's amber eyes were glowing with a light that seemed to come from within and her mouth, usually so firm and determined-looking, was soft and trembly. Veda looked, in Cindy's shrewd judgment, as if she had been quite thoroughly kissed.

"You look as if you'd been smooching in a quiet corner of the Fair," Cindy commented.

"We were," Veda said dreamily, tossing her handbag on the day bed.

"Wil Holland is a nice person," said Torre, "and he's from your home town and all. But I do think you should be careful, Veda. He might get ideas."

"He got ideas," Veda said happily. "I didn't give them to him. He got his ideas all by himself."

"Well, Torre is right," said Cindy. "You should be a little careful about going overboard for anyone like Wil Holland, though I admit he is terribly good-looking. But only a salesman—"

"He isn't a salesman," Veda said, as she kicked off her shoes.

"You told me he was a salesman," Torre said in surprise.

"I know I did," Veda said, smiling brilliantly at both her roommates. "But he isn't."

"This suspense is killing me," Cindy said languidly. "If he isn't a salesman, what does he do? Or is he one of the great army of the unemployed?"

Veda sat on the day bed and began to take off her stockings. Her hair fell in soft wings over her face as she answered:

"Wil is self-employed, you might say. Anyhow, although I appreciate your advice, girls, it comes a little late."

Cindy was standing as if frozen, watching Veda. "Is that an engagement ring you're wearing?" she demanded.

Veda held out her left hand, where a pear-shaped diamond seemed to gather all the light of the room into its flashing brilliance. "Wil Holland and I are engaged to be married," she said softly. "Isn't it wonderful?"

Cindy came over and took Veda's hand in her's, and then looked closely at the ring. As something of an expert on diamonds, Cindy knew that she was looking at a perfect gem, cut and set to perfection. She also knew that Veda did not understand what a fabulous diamond she was wearing and perhaps did not even care.

"There must be a lot of money in seeds," Cindy said, when at last she could speak. "If he owns that seed company, every flower he grows must be worth its weight in gold."

Veda looked at her so compassionately Cindy thought she would scream. "The seed company is only a subsidiary," Veda explained. "Wil heads a lot of companies, and he's a consultant, too—he's a soil engineer, he told me."

"You mean he's a millionaire?" demanded Cindy.

"Maybe." Veda shrugged. "I don't know, and I couldn't care less."

Chapter 12

Torre was surprised the next morning when she came into the office to find her grandfather sitting in Nick Tyler's chair. He was a distinguished-looking gentleman, Torre thought again, as she had that first day she had seen him in the office. His white hair was thin but carefully combed, and his shrewd blue eyes twinkled behind his sparkling nose glasses. His complexion was a healthy pink, and he looked every inch the founder of the Sealtight Siding Corporation.

"Good morning, sir," said Torre, with pretended nervousness. "Are you my new boss?"

"I am," Simon Sherrill said severely, apparently enjoying her game of pretense. "You will find it a very different matter working for me, young lady, from working for an indulgent executive like Nick Tyler."

"Has Nick been fired?" Torre asked, suddenly aware that her grandfather did not sound as if he were kidding.

"He hasn't been fired, but he's leaving," Simon

Sherrill said. "Come over here and kiss your grandfather good morning, and then you'd better sit down while I get you caught up on the latest company news."

Torre did as she was told. As she sat beside the desk where ordinarily she sat down when taking dictation from Nick Tyler, she was amazed to find she had a hollow feeling—as if she had stepped off the edge of reality and were floating in space. Surely her grandfather could not mean that Nick Tyler was actually leaving the firm. But it was part of the strangeness of the whole situation that she should be seeing her grandfather, not as the lovable Gander she had always known, but as a stern business executive whom she did not dare to question.

"You may not know it, my dear," Simon Sherrill said with great dignity, "but I am considered an excellent judge of men in the business world. When I hire a young man, I don't look only at what he can do while he is still young and untrained. I look for the potential."

"Slim Johnson," murmured Torre.

"Slim Johnson!" her grandfather exclaimed. "What do you know about him?"

"I met him once; he said he knew you." Torre almost giggled, remembering the man from downstairs in the red and white bathrobe with a blob of plaster on his head. "He isn't important. Tell me about Nick."

"Oh, yes, Nick Tyler. Well, I knew when I hired him that he would go on to a bigger job. But meantime it didn't hurt him to get some experience, practical experience, in the building of houses. I knew he wanted to be an architect, but there's nothing like the objective point of view to be gained in the advertising department of this corporation." Simon Sherrill sighed and then went on:

"Nick Tyler was even smarter than I thought. I would have liked him to stay here another year, but this job is opening up in South America, and he really has a chance to practice some of his ideas about architecture in a country where he will not be hampered by traditional forms. He is a brilliant young man, although I suppose he looks different to a pretty young thing like you. You're probably more interested in the way he dances."

"I suppose you've picked out the man who will take over his job here?" asked Torre flatly.

"Oh, yes, there's a man in Buffalo who has been wanting to come to New York for some time," Simon Sherrill assured her briskly. "He's older than Tyler—well seasoned."

"It'll be different from working for Nick," sighed Torre.

"But you won't want to stay, will you, after Nick leaves? He took good care of you—you'll miss that."

"What a funny thing to say, Gander!" exclaimed Torre. "Nick didn't have to take care of me. I took care of myself."

"But Tyler found a suitable apartment for you and saw you settled in," her grandfather reminded her.

"Of course. Why shouldn't he? He was on the spot here; he knew New York. Finding an apartment for me didn't take much effort or initiative, did it?"

"My dear, Nick has been looking out for you right along, ever since you've been in New York, even if you didn't realize it." Simon Sherrill smiled benignly at his granddaughter. "The way I see it, with Nick gone, I could never agree to let you stay here alone in the city."

"But my career! I'm really furthering it, Gander."

"You can come back to Buffalo and take a few courses in architecture. I admit you have learned a lot about business methods here, but there's no reason for you to stay longer."

"Oh, Gander, don't be stubborn!" cried Torre. "You're a darling sweet Gander and I'd love to go home with you, only—"

"Only what? You'll be lonely without Nick to take you around town down here. Have you thought of that? He has been showing you the Fair and all that kind of thing, hasn't he?"

"Yes, we've looked at a few buildings together and talked about their structure," said Torre. "But Nick isn't the only man I've dated, Gander. I've had loads of other dates."

Simon Sherrill gazed at her in alarm. "That makes

me more determined than ever to have you back in Buffalo, where I can keep an eye on you," he said. "Living all my yourself—"

"But, Gander, you've met my roommates; you know what nice, clever girls they are. We can look after ourselves. I tell you what. Why don't you come around to the apartment and see how comfortable we are and how Reba and Sam Waters take care of us just as if they were relatives or something? It's such a good neighborhod, too. You never hear of any holdups."

"I'm leaving tonight on the midnight plane," said Simon Sherrill.

"Well, stop in on your way to the airport and see for yourself," begged Torre. "You didn't really expect me to leave today, did you?"

"Well, no," her grandfather admitted. "Nick Tyler will be around here for a couple more weeks, and I wouldn't want to deprive him of his secretary just as he's winding up the job. But it's something I want you to think about. We can talk about this again. But I'd like to see your apartment, since you've invited me so earnestly, honey. I'll stop in on my way to the airport. Right now, I have to leave for a conference. Nick will be in soon, and you can get on with your work."

The office seemed quite lonely after her grandfather had gone. There were a few letters she had not done the day before, and Torre took infinite pains with each one. She was proud of the copies she laid on Nick's desk for his signature, but at the same time they seemed to her the dullest possible communications, and certainly not worth the effort she had put into them.

Finally Torre just sat before her typewriter staring with unseeing eyes at the colorful poster offered by the Sealtight Siding Corporation which decorated one wall of Nick's offce. For the first time since she had come to New York, Torre felt a definite let-down. She wondered if she had not been kidding herself with the thought that at last she was really living, really earning her own way.

After all, what did she have? A job with an indulgent boss who would soon be leaving. So she would have a job with a "seasoned" boss who might be hard to please. Other than that, she shared an apartment with two girls who were companionable but whose interests were, of course, centered in themselves. More than that, Veda was already engaged and in all probability would be too concerned with plans for her coming wedding to give much time or interest to maintaining the apartment for roommates she was soon to lose.

Almost as if she had conjured her roommates out of thin air, the phone rang and Veda's voice was saying apologetically:

"Torre darling, Wil is taking me out to the Fair tonight for dinner. We won't be late, but I thought you might like to get something to eat before you go to the apartment. We haven't a thing in the icebox—not even a quart of milk."

"I'll get a hamburger before I come home," Torre said without enthusiasm. She was feeling quite sorry for herself, although she realized that Veda, as a girl who had just become engaged, was surely above keeping her mind on groceries.

"Grandfather said he would stop by the apartment tonight," Torre added, "on his way out to the airport. About ten o'clock, I imagine."

"Oh," Veda said cheerfully, "I do want your grandfather to see our place."

When she had hung up, Torre again returned to her own gloomy thoughts. She could see now quite clearly that because she had come to New York during the year when the World's Fair opened, she had been dazzled by the gayety and beauty and fun packed into those acres on Long Island. It was like one perpetual house party, Torre was thinking, where your fellow guests were members of the international set in the true sense of the word. The World's Fair created an atmosphere of fiesta which completely transformed the routine of daily living.

It was all right for Cindy Lamson, Torre thought resentfully, to feel no let-down, even though their trio might be broken up by Veda's forthcoming marriage. Cindy's job was wholly concerned with the Fair; she was a part of it, in a way. Anyhow, Cindy was the type to keep the spotlight of glamour always focused on herself. If she did not have a job with the World's Fair, she would return to her work as a professional model. And no matter whether or not she married for money, as was her avowed intention, she would always keep herself the center of masculine attraction.

In a way, Torre was thinking, Cindy and Jac Millet were much alike. She could not picture them being married to each other. But she could picture them meeting as they had in New York and going to the World's Fair; she could see them in Paris lingering over the books and flowers on the carts along the Seine; she could see them at a formal ball at the American Embassy in London. But she could not see them as a domesticated husband and wife team. Neither one was the type. When the phone rang again, Torre told herself:

This must be Jac. The minute I start to think of someone, I hear from him. She said hello in an almost lyrical fashion, but it was not Jac. It was Nick Tyler, and he seemed annoyed.

"I'm coming back to the office in ten minutes. Will you still be there?"

"Where else would I be?" Torre asked flippantly. "It's only four-fifteen."

"I thought you might be going back to Buffalo," Nick said in a surly tone.

"You thought wrong," said Torre perversely. "I suspect you were talking to Grandfather."

"Never mind. I'll talk to you when I see you." He banged the receiver, and Torre, puzzled by his odd behavior, had no recourse but to hang up herself. Perhaps his temper would have improved by the time he got to the office, she thought, as she went over to his desk and made sure that everything was in perfect order. At any rate, she felt better; she was glad there would be an opportunity to talk with him.

His temper had not improved, Torre noted as he stalked into the office, threw her a greeting, sat down at his desk and signed the letters she had left there without even reading them. Torre resolved she would not be the first one to speak.

As she picked up the letters and took them back to her own desk to fold and put them in their envelopes, Nick apparently realized he was behaving in a strange fashion.

"I've been talking to the guy who wants me to go down to South America. I suppose your grandfather told you all about it?"

"Grandfather did mention it," Torre said coolly. "But I don't know why you should bite my head off for that reason. Frankly, I think you are just anti-social."

Nick grinned up at her. "I like the job, you understand," he said hastily, "but I am worried about you." As Torre looked at him in surprise mixed with resentment, he added:

"You can't be left alone here in New York. There are

too many wolves. I know you don't want to go back to Buffalo, but I don't see what else you can do for the moment. I'll have to fly down to Rio in the next week or two, and when I come back, it will only be to wind up my work here. I'd like you to stay on as long as I do, but I'd feel very much better if I knew you were back with your grandfather."

"Whoever appointed you my private watch dog?" Torre asked. "Gander told me he had asked you to look out for me, but I don't believe he meant you were to put me in a concentration camp where no one is allowed to speak to me. You say there are too many wolves in New York. I'm not exactly a child, Nick Tyler, and it could be I like wolves."

"Name of Jac?" Nick asked with raised eyebrows.

"Name of anyone," Torre said angrily. "I will not be treated like a retarded child and told when to smile and when to frown. And I'm *not* going back to Buffalo."

"Your grandfather will have something to say about that," Nick said with finality. "Meanwhile, you have made it very hard for me to tell you how much I have enjoyed working with you and how I wish it could go on a little longer and how I was hoping that this new job—anxious as I am to get it—didn't have to be accepted in such a rush. . . ."

"Skip it," Torre said tersely. "And speaking of Grandfather, he's going to stop by the apartment tonight on his way to the airport. I guess he's checking up to see that you did your job right in getting me the apartment."

"You're in an impossible mood," Nick accused her. "I'll take this up with you tomorrow."

"Me impossible?" Torre said hotly. But Nick had already banged out of the office, and the telephone was ringing.

"Hello, Torre? What's the matter with my girl?" Jac asked as she picked up the phone.

"I'm mad clear through," Torre told him, "but I didn't know it showed."

"Mad at me, sweet? Don't be, because I want to take you to dinner tonight. Not at the Fair, but a little further out on the island. Friends of mine are off to Europe, and they want us to stop in and say *bon voyage*."

"I promised I'd be back at the apartment by ten o'clock. . . ."

"Plenty of time," Jac Millet said cheerfully. "This is one of those affairs where you can come and go as you please. I'm hoping for my own sake you won't make it too short a visit. Maybe we could sit and hold hands awhile and watch the ocean. They've got a private beach."

"As long as I get back by ten," Torre said, evading a direct answer. "And, Jac, thank you for asking me. I was feeling mightly low and unwanted."

Chapter 13

Out in the street, everything was bright with the
golden light of the late afternoon sun. Torre had a
happy sense of anticipation. Jac was just the compan-
ion she needed this evening, she was thinking—deb-
onair, exciting. She looked forward to meeting a lot of
people she did not know—a group in a holiday mood,
enjoying a *bon voyage* party. For the past two weeks
she had been too much concerned with her work and
various problems, including those of her roommates,
and yes, Nick Tyler. It would do her good to have a
complete change from everyone she knew and their
affairs.

It was something of a disappointment not to find Jac
waiting outside the entrance of the office building. She
stood for a second looking around, but he was not in
sight. Her glance strayed to the curb, and she noted
automatically that the white convertible standing there

was upholstered in a very pretty shade of blue leather and that the chromium trim apparently had been polished not more than an hour before. Then all at once she saw the driver. It was Jac. He was grinning broadly as he leaned over and opened the door on her side.

"Why didn't you tell me you were going to steal a car?" Torre laughed as she settled herself beside him. "We've always taken a taxi before this."

"How do you know it isn't my car?" Jac asked, driving it smoothly into the traffic and heading crosstown.

"Because no one could have a car as beautiful as this without driving it all the time," Torre said promptly. "This is the car I always wanted, but my grandfather thought it was a little flashy. I sold my car before I came to New York," she added.

"You are a very smart girl," Jac said, as he sent the convertible skimming over the Queensborough Bridge. "You are right. This car doesn't belong to me, but I didn't steal it. I borrowed it from one of the men at the Consulate. Apart from the difficulty of hiring a taxi to go thirty miles out on Long Island and then asking the driver to wait around while you enjoy a party and then to drive you back, I wouldn't want to arrive at the Meredith estate in anything but the best."

"A terribly snazzy couple?" Torre asked.

"Dick and Poopsie? Yes. You can say that again. Every so often one of her relatives dies and she gets another quarter of a million. Then they take off for a cruise or an African safari or whatever they feel like at the moment."

"I gather Dick is not in the money himself," Torre observed. "You know that old saying: the man who marries for money earns it."

"It isn't hurting Dick any to earn it," Jac answered, and Torre was surprised to hear a note of envy in his voice. "Poopsie is a beautiful girl, and she couldn't trail around all over the world without an escort. Dick is young, handsome and healthy; she gets her money's worth."

"What an odd way to look at marriage," Torre said.

Jac glanced at her quickly, then said:

"I was just giving you the background on this couple; it doesn't really concern us in the least. But I am concerned about what you said over the phone: that you had to get back to the apartment by ten o'clock. I'm going to see to it that you won't want to go back. You'll be having too much fun."

Torre thought of telling him about her grandfather stopping by the apartment that night and then decided against it. She had spent so many years being where she was told to be at the time she was told to be there that it was pleasant to contemplate a moment of rebellion. She could even picture herself phoning Gander before he left the hotel, and saying airily:

"I'm having such a good time, Grandfather, I won't be back in town until after you leave. You can see the apartment some other time."

"What are you grinning to yourself about?" Jac asked her. "You must be terribly pleased with your thoughts."

Torre assured him she was only dreaming and actually was enjoying the drive along the smooth highway on a sunlit evening. As they went farther out onto the island, she thought she could detect the tang of salt in the air, although when she mentioned it Jac shook his head. The Meredith estate, he told her, was on the North Shore of Long Island, and they had a private beach which bordered on Long Island Sound.

Dick Meredith had been only a clerk at the Consulate when Jac first knew him, Jac said idly, his long brown fingers on the wheel looking particularly competent to Torre, who felt you could judge a man by the way he handled a car. She did not like the too careless grip that some men affected to show how expert they were, or the extra cautious grasp of some men who showed their concern for a dented fender. Jac's hands rested lightly on the wheel, but their touch was sure, and the car responded as if he were holding the reins of a spirited horse.

With only an occasional word from Torre, Jac sketched in a picture of Dick, the perennial blond football hero who had met and married a wealthy girl without conscious effort. As Jac talked, Torre reflected that she had been quite right about him and Cindy: they were alike. They both put a high price on material gain, and romance was incidental for them.

The traffic was thinning out now, and Jac had turned off the main highway to what had evidently been a well traveled road some years before. Torre had been so interested in what he was saying that she realized with a sudden shock they had been driving quite a while.

"You said the Meredith place was thirty miles away?" she questioned.

"As the crow flies," Jac said coolly. "I never had a chance to clock it before. Anyhow, it's only about ten miles farther."

Torre did not like it. She would not have come so far out on the island if Jac had not told her it was only thirty miles away. She forgot about her former plan of calling her grandfather and saying she was delayed. Of course she would not do that! It would be childish. Even if they just had time to go into the Meredith's and stay for an hour, she must make sure that she was back in New York by ten o'clock.

The road ran between high stone walls and ornamental fences half hidden in shrubbery. There were very few cars on the road now, and the rooftops Torre could glimpse among the trees were only indications of the houses that were undoubtedly there.

"These people surely like privacy, don't they?" she remarked. "I imagine that the homes on the other side of
these fences are quite handsome. I wish I could see them.
I'm interested in architecture, you know."

"You are!" Jac was genuinely surprised. "Why does
the granddaughter of Simon Sherrill want to go mess-
ing around with a lot of drainpipes and foundations and
cement building blocks?"

"You might say it's in the blood," Torre said lightly.
"Grandfather wanted to be an architect, but he had to
settle for making insulation instead."

"And for making a lot of money, too," Jac said dryly.
"Well, here we are. I'll just get out and open the
gate. . . ."

Almost before she realized it, Jac had stopped the
car with its nose pointed at the center of a great double
wrought-iron gate set into stone pillars on either side of
the drive.

As she watched, Jac walked forward and, with a
push, swung the huge gates back; they opened onto the
driveway with no effort. The gate had not been locked.
But neither had it been open. Torre sat speechless as
Jac came back and got into the car as if this were the
most natural thing in the world to do, drove through the
gates, stopped the car, got out again and pushed them
shut behind him.

Torre could not quite believe what was happening. The house they approached was a big, rambling affair of sandstone and stucco, with beautifully kept lawns and well-trimmed hedges. They approached from the back of the house, and an open graveled space below an unroofed terrace was a convenient parking lot. Jac drove the convertible next to the house and turned off the ignition. Then he looked at her with a smile.

"Here we are."

Torre felt a wave of anger so violent she had to get control of herself before she could even speak. She had known, of course, from the moment Jac had gotten out of the car to open the gates, that there was no *bon voyage* party going on in the house and that Dick and Poopsie Meredith, if indeed they did live there, were not at home. She managed to say at last:

"Your friends have already gone to Europe, haven't they?"

"They left last week."

"Why are the gates unlocked when they are closed?"

"The road is patroled by private cops. The gates are open in case of fire or in case a prowler takes refuge in the house. Saves having a caretaker live here. Are you angry with me?"

"Not angry; just annoyed. I told you I wanted to be back in New York early. You said this was a party where we could come and go at any time and that it was only a short distance from New York. Instead, it's a good hour's drive. There is no party and therefore no reason we should have come all this way. In fact, I have no intention of even going inside."

"Afraid?" Jac's voice held an undertone of scorn.

"Of course I'm not afraid," Torre said hotly. "But I can't see the reason behind this elaborate buildup to a silly let-down."

"I suppose it is a let-down for you," Jac said, and he sounded really penitent. "But there is something to be said on my side, too. I have seen you only at the World's Fair, against a background of color and lights and excitement. I liked what I saw. But I did want to get to know you a little better. When Dick went abroad, he gave me the keys to the house and told me I could come out here for a few hours any time, stay overnight if I wanted to, or for a long weekend, use his bathing trunks and go swimming. The way Dick put it, I'd be doing him a favor if I did come out here occasionally just to make sure everything was okay. But of course if you think this is some sort of trap laid by a villain in an old-fashioned movie, we'll go right back to New York."

Torre felt ashamed of herself. Jac did not have any place where he could entertain, and although it had been foolish of him to lie about a *bon voyage* party in order to get her out here, there was no great harm done. The house itself did not seem frightening. In fact, from this angle it did not seem quite as large as Gander's home in Buffalo, the place where she had been living while she was growing up. It must have been built in about the same era—roughly before World War I. Anyway, since they were there, she might as well act like a sophisticated person and not like a timid schoolgirl.

"Of course we'll go inside," Torre said, on a sudden impulse. She opened the door and jumped out of the car.

Jac looked at her with a brilliant smile. "That's my girl," he said joyously. Then he reached over and took the key out of the ignition. Instantly, her former misgivings came back.

"Why are you taking the keys out of the car?" she asked sharply.

"Oh, for Pete's sake!" Jac sounded disgusted. "The key to this house is on my key ring. Are you sure you don't expect me to strangle you, once we get inside?"

"Sorry."

They walked around the house to the front door, which was of dark wood like the timber trim of the outside walls. It was a type of architecture with which Torre was familiar. She did not particularly care for it. It was pseudo-English manor style and seemed out of place in this location. But she knew exactly how it would look inside.

There was a large, elaborate iron door handle, but

only for decoration; the small key Jac carried fitted into a modern lock just below it. As he opened the door, Torre saw that she was right.

A large central hallway had archways right and left leading to living room and dining room. Straight ahead an oak stairway wound up to the second story. There were oriental rugs on the floor, and the furnishings were not only comfortable and in good taste, but quite luxurious. Jac had recovered his good humor. He pushed the door open wide and, with a sudden laugh, caught her up in his arms and carried her into the hall.

He was remarkably strong. His arms, as they held her, were like steel bands, and his dark eyes, glinting now with amusement, looked directly into hers.

"Aren't you getting ahead of yourself?" Torre said with a smile. "There's a marriage ceremony supposed to come before you carry a girl over the threshold. And I think the house is supposed to be yours; not borrowed."

He lowered her gently until she was standing on the floor, but kept his arms tightly around her. His voice was unexpectedly husky, and he was no longer laughing.

"You don't know the effect you have on me, Torre. Every time I see you I have a feeling you are not quite real. There can't be anyone quite so beautiful, quite so graceful, quite so charming as a girl named Torre Sherrill. She must be just a dream that a poor fool named

Jac Millet created because he was so lonely."

Without meaning to, Torre took his face in both her hands and kissed him gently on the lips. "You are a sweet fellow, Jac," she said, "but you mustn't glamorize me so much. I'm just an ordinary run-of-the-mill working girl—one of thousands. At the moment this working girl could do with a long, cold drink of water. You wouldn't by any chance know where the kitchen is?"

Jac released her and, holding her hand, led her through a shadowy dining room, a long butler's pantry with stainless steel counters and on into a modern kitchen in copper and turquoise blue. Torre went at once to the sink and turned on the faucet. She opened the cupboard above and took out one of the glasses.

"Take one out for me, too," Jac said. He had gone over and was squatting before a low wooden cabinet with a lock like that on a safe door. He spun the dial a few times and then swung the door back. Inside was a well-stocked cellarette.

"Name your poison," Jac said, reaching in and taking out a bottle. "Me, I like the brand of bourbon which Dick has been drinking ever since he was in the money. But if you'd rather have Scotch—"

Torre thought fast as she sipped her glass of water. She had been offered liquor before, and it was simple enough to refuse. But it wasn't only the offer of a drink that was wrong now; it was the whole situation. She was in a spot, Torre knew, and she had to try to figure some way to get out of it. As she continued to remain silent, Jac repeated impatiently:

"Well, what'll it be? After the third drink, I guarantee you won't care whether you get back to New York by ten o'clock or not."

Chapter 14

Jac Millet, his eyes glittering and with the air of one who has just completed a difficult coup, was not the suave, restrained admirer who had given her several enjoyable evenings at the Fair, and Torre had the feeling that she was in a room with a stranger.

There was one thought uppermost in her mind. She had to get away. She could not use the car because Jac, after he had let himself into the house, had dropped the key ring into his pocket. But she could run down the drive; she could get onto the road. Perhaps Jac would come after her, but he would not dare create a scene in the middle of a public highway. If she could reach a phone—

Jac had put the bottle of Scotch and the bottle of bourbon on the kitchen table and was opening and shutting cupboard doors with impatience, "Where the devil do they keep their shot glasses?" he grumbled, half to himself.

"Perhaps they are in the pantry," Torre said, and was glad her voice sounded normal and unafraid. "I'll go look." She went through the swinging door hastily, fearful that he would try to stop her. Instead he called out to her:

"Never mind. I've found one. I'm looking for a tray now, but I think I know where the housekeeper has them hidden. Go on into the living room; I'll be with you in a minute."

"Okay."

Torre moved swiftly through the dining room and into the hall. She made no sound as she opened the front door and started around the house. Of course, Jac in the kitchen might be able to see her from the window —if he happened to look out—but it was a chance she would have to take. If she were lucky he would not look up but would continue to fix the tray with the glasses and the liquor. Torre knew he did not dream she would walk out on him. She thought perhaps it was the first time Jac had ever had that experience. Nor did he think of her walking. With the keys to the car in his pocket, he might expect she would try to persuade him to drive her back to town.

And she could not walk those forty or fifty miles. That was true. She reached the wrought-iron gate and pushed one side open just enough to slide through; then she closed it after herself. She had to find a phone and ask Nick to come to get her. It did not occur to her to call anyone else. Somehow, for all Nick's truculence and his patronizing attitude that afternoon, he was always the man one could turn to in moments of crisis.

Torre reached the road, which stretched right and left in both directions. And in both directions it was completely empty. She glanced at her watch. It was eight-thirty, and already the shadows heralding the evening were gathering among the bushes beside the road. Once it was dark, this would be a frightening experience. Even now, Torre shivered. She resolutely turned away from New York.

She did not remember having passed a gas station for many miles before they reached the Meredith estate. Therefore, she reasoned, there must be a gas station quite near if she continued on down the road.

And where there is a gas station there is a telephone, Torre told herself, and wished she had not put on spike heels for the evening's date. They ought to keep their road in better condition. It's disgraceful, that's what it is —the way the macadam is broken and cracked—oops!

Her heel caught in an unexpected depression, and Torre forced herself to slow down. It did not pay to hurry and risk spraining an ankle. The road turned abruptly, and Torre halted, staring ahead in dismay. On her right was a high wall of squared stone with barbed wire visible along the top. Now the road was close to the Sound on the left; she could see the water only a short distance away. For almost a mile there was no big estate, no high stone wall on that side; there was only one ramshackle building. But it looked beautiful to Torre. There was a gas pump in front of it.

The building did not improve in appearance as she drew closer; the gas pump looked as if it might have been disconnected, and the few cars that were drawn up in front of the door were of uncertain vintage. The one dirty window had a neon sign advertising beer, and in a lean-to at the side there was a hand-lettered sign saying simply: "Nite Crawlers."

Torre giggled to herself. Maybe I'm a nite crawler, she thought. But the idea brought no comfort. It was a most uninviting shack, and she had no illusions about the type of men who would choose it for an hour of convivial conversation over a glass of beer. But there should be a telephone.

She was right, Torre discovered, as she opened the door and walked into a small, smoke-filled room, with a bar along one side. There were three men sitting at a table, all in work clothes, although Torre could not imagine what type of work it was that required such a nondescript wardrobe. The bartender, also, appeared to be one of the fraternity; his plaid shirt was quite dirty and had lost many of its buttons.

Torre had been prepared in some measure for the scene that met her eyes. But it was evident the men were utterly unprepared for her. A dead silence fell on the room, and there was only one small whisper of sound as the one man at the bar put his glass of beer down without taking a drink.

"I beg your pardon," Torre said a little breathlessly, "but may I use your phone?"

"The phone?" The bartender stared at her as if he had never heard of the invention. But a coarse, unshaven man with bold brown eyes grinned and showed his broken teeth.

"You heard the lady, Chuck. Don'cha know what a phone is? It's that thing hanging on the wall back there. I never seen you use it."

"Of course I know what a phone is," the bartender said with wounded dignity. "But I got all those beer cases piled up in front of it. The guy was supposed to pick them up last Tuesday. . . . Don't you think you'd better go get a phone somewhere else, miss?"

A thin, bleary-eyed man who was sitting at the table and who also did not believe in razors looked up and said chidingly:

"Now, Chuck, where's your chivaree? Anyway, don't you see the girlie is walking home from a date? She ain't got no way to go round looking for a phone."

Torre gave the man a grateful smile and was surprised to see him shrink back almost as if he were afraid of her. "Thank you; I would appreciate using the telephone here," she said. "I want to call New York."

"New York!" objected the bartender. "That's a toll call."

"I'll reverse the charges," Torre said hastily.

Grumbling under his breath, the bartender, Chuck, led her over to a dark corner where the beer cases were indeed piled high. She forced herself to say brightly, as she glimpsed the phone hanging on the wall.

"This is just like a telephone booth." Chuck grunted and turned back toward the bar, and suddenly Torre realized she had left her purse in the Meredith kitchen. "Could you—I mean, please, will you give me a dime so that I can get the operator? It will be returned to me, you know, when I reverse the charges."

"Give the lady a dime, Chuck," the bold-eyed man said with a coarse laugh. "It ain't every day you get a visit from royalty in this dump. How'd ja get away from the palace guards, Your Highness?"

The man in the room joined in the general laughter; evidently the bold-eyed character was the wit of the gathering, Torre thought resentfully. But Chuck produced the dime, and Torre, by dint of complete concentration, managed to give the operator Nick's phone number at the apartment he shared with another man. "And reverse the charges," Torre said loudly and clearly, for Chuck's benefit.

It had not occurred to her until the phone rang and rang and rang again that Nick would not be at home. She looked beyond the sign of the dirty window and saw that outside it was now almost completely dark. The unshaded bulb above the bar made the room bright by contrast and cast unkind shadows on the faces of the five men. When there was no longer any use hanging on, Torre hung up slowly, and the dime clinked back in the return slot. She picked it up and walked over to the bar.

"Thank you," she said in a flat voice, but Chuck did not pick it up.

"Maybe you could call somebody else, miss," he began sympathetically. But the door banged open, and Jac Millet crossed to the bar and took hold of Torre's wrist in an iron grip.

"What the devil do you mean running off like that?" he demanded furiously. "I didn't think you were such an infant."

"I have to get back to New York," Torre explained, feeling suddenly tired. "Grandfather is going to stop by the apartment on his way to the airport about ten o'clock."

Jac looked at his wristwatch and swore under his breath. "We can make it," he said. "Come on. Why didn't you tell me you were meeting your grandfather at ten o'clock?"

"You said I wouldn't care about going back after I'd had some drinks," Torre quavered. But she made no resistance as Jac pulled her toward the door. The men in the tavern maintained a respectful silence, as if they were watching a scene in a play. Only the bold-eyed man recovered himself quickly enough to say:

"So long, Your Highness. Drop in to see us again when you want to use the phone."

They were halfway back to New York before Torre spoke to the man beside her, who was driving skillfully, taking advantage of every break in the traffic to gain a few minutes' time. Jac had never changed in his angry attitude toward her, and Torre began to resent it more and more. If anyone were angry, she should be the one to claim the privilege. But Jac was acting as if the whole fiasco had been her fault. Torre thought of several comments to make, but what she finally said was:

"I hope you are thoroughly ashamed of yourself."

"No; why should I be?" Jac bit off the words. "I made a play for you, and in my opinion you asked for it. So," Jac shrugged, "I lost out. You pushed the panic button."

"I don't know what you mean when you say I asked for it. You lied to me and told me you were taking me out to a party."

"You lied to me, too, or at least you didn't tell the whole truth. You said you had to be back in New York by ten o'clock; you didn't tell me your grandfather would be waiting for you."

"What difference does it make?" Torre demanded. "You promised to get me back at ten o'clock, and you didn't ask me why I wanted to return. Whether Grandfather was coming to the apartment or whether I had told Veda I was going to be home at that time was immaterial, or should have been—to you."

"Oh, grow up!" Jac said in a disgusted tone. "I don't give a hoot what Veda thinks about me or even what she thinks about you. But your grandfather's got the money. If he once got down on me, he could make it hot at the Consulate. They take a dim view there of anyone who antagonizes our senior and wealthy citizens."

"Yes, Grandfather would have been angry," Torre admitted, "and when you talked about holding me in that empty house until it was too late to see Grandfather off on the plane, I panicked, as you said. I'd never been in a situation like that before, you see."

"No, you haven't. You've been wrapped in cotton wool so tight that you think everybody is going to watch out for you and see that you don't get in a jam. Until tonight I didn't believe you were all that naïve."

"I don't know what's gotten into everyone," Torre burst out impatiently. "I came to New York, I got a job and I held it, I am living on the money I make, and I haven't any keeper to lock me up at night or see that I don't go the wrong way on a one-way street."

"That's what you say. Actually, you've never been without a keeper. First you lived at home with your grandfather in a community where everyone knew that if anybody made one false move toward you, old Si Sherrill would put him on the torture rack. Then you came to New York, and your grandfather appointed Nick Tyler as a watchdog."

"That isn't true," said Torre, but her voice was very small. "Nick never said I couldn't go here or couldn't go there or that I couldn't go out with another man— like you, for instance."

Jac laughed as they drove over the bridge and he turned the car to go uptown.

"I didn't say Nick put on a white coat and went around with a butterfly net to catch you if you stepped out of line. But nevertheless he knew pretty well what you did with your spare time, and I imagine he knew when you went to the Fair with me. But even though he probably warned you against me, Nick knew he had a powerful ally in your own little small town conscience. He counted on it, and he was right."

"Is that bad?" Torre demanded. "I like my conscience, small town or not."

"And you don't mind Nick being a watchdog either, do you? Tell me, when you went into that dirty little joint to use the telephone, didn't you try to get Nick Tyler?"

Torre sat silent. Jac turned east, and a few seconds later he had stopped the convertible in front of her apartment house. The habit of training was strong. As she got out of the car Torre said automatically:

"Won't you come upstairs and meet Grandfather?"

Jac shook his head. "What a well-trained little girl you are. I'm surprised you didn't politely thank me for a pleasant evening. No, I won't come upstairs; and no, I don't want to meet your grandfather. I have an idea the old bandit and I would understand each other at sight. This is goodbye, Torre. I won't say, 'Take care of yourself,' because I know you will always have a dozen people to take care of you. The Number One boy, of course, will be Nick Tyler."

Torre looked at him blankly for a moment, and then she smiled radiantly before she turned to go inside.

"Goodbye, Jac, and thank you for pointing out so clearly what I was too blind to see for myself. It's true

Grandfather has always looked after me and Nick Tyler has watched over me, too, since I have been here, but I'll tell you a secret, Jac. I don't resent being watched over; I discover I really like it. In fact, I adore it, if the person who does the watching is Nick Tyler."

Upstairs, in the apartment, Simon Sherrill was saying the same thing to Nick Tyler but with a slightly different inflection.

"I thought you were watching over my granddaughter," Si Sherrill was barking irritably. "Yet here it is after ten o'clock, and Torre isn't here, you don't know where she is, and you admit she has been seeing another man behind your back. I thought you liked looking out for my granddaughter. If you weren't interested, why didn't you say so? I would have taken measures to see that she was adequately protected at all times."

"I'm in love with your granddaughter, sir," Nick said, his hands working as if he wanted to tear the town apart piece by piece until he found Torre. "I wasn't going to tell you so and I wasn't going to speak to her until I made good on the job. But now I guess we'll have to come to an understanding. She refuses to go back to Buffalo, and I can't go off to South America and leave her running around New York alone. Maybe she won't want me to worry about her any more, but I'll have to ask her."

"I think the younger generation is extremely slow," Si Sherrill said testily. "In my day we didn't waste time when we went to the Fair."

Chapter 15

Simon Sherrill jumped to his feet with an exclamation and stalked over to the window of the apartment for the fifth time in ten minutes. Nick kept his seat by the TV with difficulty. He was as anxious as the old gentleman to know why Torre was not there. But he did not believe in calling either the police or the hospitals, both of which measures Simon Sherrill had suggested.

"I knew something was wrong the minute we had to get the superintendent's wife to let us in," Simon Sherrill fumed. "I tell you Torre herself asked me to come to the apartment before I went to the airport. She must have had a premonition something would go wrong."

Nick sternly repressed an exclamation of impatience. "It's only five minutes of ten, sir," he pointed out. "Wherever Torre went after she left the office, she has probably been delayed. . . ."

"I know what time it is," Si Sherrill barked. "And I also know my granddaughter. I ought to; I brought her up ever since her parents were killed in that crash. If she makes a date, she keeps it. And she isn't late, either," he finished belligerently.

Nick again retired into silence. There was no arguing with Si Sherrill on the subject of his granddaughter. He wondered where in the world Torre had gone, anyway. She had said she would not go back to Buffalo, but surely that did not mean she would run off and get herself embroiled in some situation that would make it necessary for her to stay in New York.

"What exactly did she say to you when she left the office?" Simon Sherrill demanded, sitting on the edge of the love seat once more.

"I've told you, sir," Nick repeated, "I left the office before Torre did. She may have made a dinner date. . . ."

"Why don't you know?" Si Sherrill shot at him. "She told me she had been running around with a lot of dates. I thought you were looking after my granddaughter. She's too young and innocent to be turned loose in New York alone. I was worried because you were going away and wouldn't be around to look after her any more. But I guess anyone would do as good a job as you do."

Nick held onto his temper. "I didn't realize I was

supposed to be your granddaughter's jailer," he said. "I don't consider myself qualified to watch out for a girl with Torre's beauty and intelligence if she wants to go her own way."

"If she wants to go out with other men, I suppose you mean," Simon Sherrill said shrewdly. "What's the matter? Couldn't you give those other fellows a little competition?"

"I didn't think of it that way," Nick said humbly. "I simply fell in love with your granddaughter, sir."

"Did you speak to her yet?"

"No, sir."

"What's the matter with you? Scared?"

"Scared stiff," Nick admitted. "But I am going to ask her to marry me before I take on this new job. If she turns me down, I'll go to South America and stay there."

"What if she accepts you?"

"We'll both go to South America," Nick said with a grin. "And you, sir, can come down for a visit."

At that moment they both heard a key in the lock, and Torre, in Nick's eyes looking more beautiful than ever, stood in the doorway.

"Sorry I'm late, Gander," she apologized. "I was unavoidably detained. I went out to Long Island to a farewell party." It was true, she reflected. She had said a firm farewell to Jac Millet.

"I think you work too hard, Cindy," Rad Farnsworth said as he piloted the blonde model into the lobby of the apartment house with great solicitude. "I know you like your job, but it is a very demanding one—meeting the public all day long. Perhaps we should have gone to a quieter place to eat. . . ."

"Oh, Rad, for heaven's sake!" Cindy exclaimed. "Forget it. Occasionally I do get a headache. But that doesn't mean you have to call an ambulance and take me to the hospital." She punched the button for the third floor with vicious emphasis. "I don't believe anybody will be in yet, and we'll have a few moments to talk together."

Cindy forced herself to make the prospect sound alluring to Rad. Since she had misssed out on Wil Holland and Jac Millet had apparently found someone else, she could not afford to antagonize her only escort. In fact, she had been thinking, during the last twenty-four hours, that Rad Farnsworth's offer of a comfortable if not spectacular marriage might be acceptable. It would be fun to marry a man of wealth or the adventuresome Jac, but the year she had given herself to find a millionaire was almost over, and prospects for a brilliant marriage were fading fast.

As Cindy and Rad stepped out of the elevator, they almost collided with Torre and her grandfather and Nick. The explanations were necessarily hurried, and

Rad and Cindy had only time to thank Torre's grandfather once more for his hospitality at the Fair. Then the three were gone, and Cindy got out her key and went into the apartment.

"Torre is looking very well, isn't she?" Rad commented, as he walked over to the window. "She really has the biggest eyes I've ever seen. Don't you think so, Cindy?"

"Yes," Cindy said shortly. Then, remembering her resolve to be nicer to her only escort at the moment, she added: "Something tells me that Torre and Nick have reached an understanding—to use a quaint, old-fashioned term. And as I told you, Wil Holland has given Veda a diamond ring as big as a headlight. Of the three of us, only poor little old me is left all alone."

Oddly enough, Rad Farnsworth did not offer immediate consolation, as Cindy had expected he would. Instead, with some practicality, he told her:

"You are not alone. I am here."

"You know what I mean," Cindy said, thinking it wise to let her voice quaver a little. "I'm not talking about tonight, I'm talking about love that lasts for a lifetime. Veda and Torre have found that, I think."

"I didn't know you wanted love for a lifetime," Rad said unexpectedly.

"Every girl wants love and romance and marriage, too."

"You know how I feel about you, Cindy. You know I would have offered you marriage and devotion for a lifetime at any moment during the last year. But you always held me off. You always seemed to be looking for something I can't give you."

"What a thing to say to me!" Cindy could not have been more astonished if a rabbit had turned around and bitten her. "You know I like you, Rad. I've seen you more often than any other man ever since the Fair opened, and even six months before that."

"Yes, you went out with me," Rad said, "but I always felt I was second string. Before you came to this apartment, there was that magazine editor who liked your pictures so much, and the head of the advertising agency who got you the assignments. I guess," Rad said, with a wistful note in his voice, "there were others I probably didn't even know about."

"Is it your idea," Cindy asked sharply, "to lock me up in a house after we're married and never let me speak to another man? Because I will attract many men in the years to come, Rad, and the man I marry must understand that, and give me the freedom to enjoy my life in my own way."

"That's all right," Rad said quickly, "as long as I am the Number One man."

"My husband will be the Number One man in my life," Cindy said firmly.

"In that case," said Rad, "will you marry me?"

"In that case," retorted Cindy, "I will. But remember," she murmured, as Rad folded her in his arm, "I don't want a jealous husband."

Torre's eyes filled with tears as the plane bearing her grandfather taxied down the runway and took off. Nick's arm tightened about her shoulders, and she leaned against him for a brief second. She was tired. The evening had been a long one, but already its unpleasantness was beginning to fade into the background.

"How about a cup of coffee?"

"You'll spend more than the price of a cup of coffee on me," Torre warned him. "What with one thing and another, I didn't get any dinner."

"One thing or another being a date with Jac Millet, I suppose," Nick said as he settled her in a cab and gave the driver the name of a steak house which Torre knew was famous for its charcoal-broiled steaks.

"What are you—clairvoyant?" Torre demanded.

"No," said Nick, "but it figured. I remember a pair of jade earrings. Do you want to tell me about tonight's date?"

Torre shrugged. "Not particularly. It was unpleasant, but it's over now."

"Good!" Nick commented, and said no more until they were seated in the restaurant and steaks had been ordered and were, they were assured, on the fire. Even then, their conversation was casual and impersonal until the meal had been served and the steaks eaten with enjoyment. Torre sipped at her coffee and said reflectively:

"Next time you will think twice before you ask me to dinner. I surely put away a meal that would have satisfied a stevedore."

"I'm glad you enjoyed it," Nick said formally. "But to go back to what we were saying—you went out with Jac Millet and were late getting back to the apartment. What in the world did you two do during those five hours? Were you at the Fair?"

"It was only four hours," Torre objected. "What we did was drive out—a way out—on Long Island to the home of Dick and Poopsie Meredith. They were supposed to be having a bon voyage party."

"Supposed to be?"

"Poopsie and Dick sailed last week. We were a little late."

"Oh." Nick said nothing more for a moment. Then he began: "About your staying in New York—now that I'm about to go to South America and your grandfather has gone back to Buffalo, I think you might reconsider returning there yourself. I know you are doing all right here, but New York can be a mighty lonesome place for a girl as young and full of life as you are."

Torre sighed a mock sigh. "Perhaps I agree with you about its being lonesome here for me. I wonder if I'd like it down in South America?"

"What changed your mind about New York being the only place in the world for you?"

"Oh, one thing and another," said Torre airily.

"The *bon voyage* party that didn't come off, maybe?"

"Oh, no," said Torre, her eyes luminous. "It was something Gander whispered to me just before he kissed me goodbye."

"What did he say?"

"That's for me to know and you to find out." Torre shrugged flippantly. "If I may suggest it, I think we ought to get out of here. Somewhere there must be a lovely lake, with the moon shining on the water. . . ."

"Would you settle for a hansom cab twice around Central Park, in slow motion?" Nick asked.

Torre nodded enthusiastically. "I think that's a gorgeous idea."

"What are we waiting for?" asked Nick, grinning at her. "You know what? I know now what your grandfather whispered to you. He told you I loved you." His voice was soft. "Haven't you something to tell me, too?"

"Let's find that hansom cab first," Torre said.

"It's funny," Veda said to Wil, as they sat before "their" fountain at the World's Fair, "how one little decision which doesn't seem important at the time can shape your life."

"Like, for instance?" Wil questioned, fondling her hand and turning it so that the diamond ring caught the lights around them.

"Like when I decided I didn't want to live in a hotel, and I wrote Dad and asked him what he thought of my renting an apartment and advertising for out-of-town girls to share it with me. If I hadn't had the apartment, and if Cindy Lamson and Torre Sherrill hadn't happened to become my two roommates, maybe all these wonderful things that have happened to me wouldn't have happened."

"There's one thing sure though—I would have found you wherever in the world you were," said Wil Holland. "Some things are just meant to be. Perhaps you might not have left Kansas City. But then I am sure I would have gone back there, and sooner or later I would have met you and fallen in love with you."

"But Jack Simmons, your friend, is in the New York office," Veda objected. "How would he have introduced us? He never came to the Right-O! Cereal Company in Kansas City," she added teasingly.

"I have other friends besides Jack Simmons, a lot of them in Kansas City. I wouldn't have needed anyone, though. I have my own private radar system," Wil said solemnly. "When it comes to love—to loving you, that is—we are on the same wave length. We couldn't have missed."

"You sound like one of those marvelous new machines in the IBM Pavilion." Veda giggled.

"Those are marvelous machines all right," agreed Wil, "but automation will never replace romance."

"You're so right," Veda whispered.